# Call It Our Village

by

Margaret L.Y. Soleyn

**Call It Our Village**

By Margaret L. Y. Soleyn

© 2021 Margaret L.Y. Soleyn

ISBN: 9798713374860

All rights reserved. No part of this publication may be reproduced, distributed, or transmitted in any form or by any means, including photocopying, recording, or other electronic or mechanical methods, without the prior written permission of the publisher, except in the case of brief quotations embodied in critical reviews and certain other noncommercial uses permitted by copyright law.

For my children

## *Chapter One*

At the first sound of the menacing growl, I merely made a hasty glance in that direction to ascertain the proximity of the animal, then I was flying downhill, determined not to be caught. My sister's command, "Don't run!" wafted eerily in my wake as the enthusiastic panting of the dog at my heels propelled me downhill at greater speed. On arriving at the embankment above the road, I took one desperate leap. Airborne, I heard the ripping of my skirt tail behind me. I landed on both feet, and barely sparing a glance right and left dashed across the road and into the safety of my godmother's yard. Up the stairs I raced and through the open door, gasping.

"Vaughna Craigg! What happened? Where's Dell?" Nennie asked, concern in her voice as she held me and peered around the door frame.

"Look me here. I told her not to run, but she never bothers with me," Dell responded. She was holding the small basket with the fruits and some provision we were taking home from "up the hill." Fruits, mostly mangoes, grew in abundance on family lands on the hillside on the other side of the village, but the tenants on the land were not always forthcoming with the produce.

From time to time, they would send a message for us to come collect 'some things.' I didn't even remember letting go of my half of the handle of the basket.

"So what happened? She sounds as though the devil himself were chasing her," Nennie observed. One hand was over my vibrating chest as though to prevent my heart from breaking through my chest cavity while the other soothingly rubbed my back.

"Mrs. Harry's dog barked, and she took off." And with the voice of the elderly wise added, "Granny always says that no one can chase you if you're not running."

"Well, that might just be so, but sit down and let me get you something to drink. Lord, have mercy!" Nennie soon handed us glasses of her special limeade as Miss Lou her lifelong friend and companion looked on. Before darkness fell, we were on our way home again.

My godmother whom we both called "Nennie" had no children of her own, but she had several godchildren. She made sure that she had some trinket for each of us on our birthdays and at Christmas. Her house was full of all sorts of interesting items and I loved to just walk from one shiny polished table or shelf to another, looking at the variety of curios placed on little doilies there. And I loved my Nennie. She was my idea of a lady, tall and neither boney nor fat. She was pretty too, and she had the prettiest hair. It was thick and grey. Once she caught me looking intently as Miss Lou combed it and told me I could touch it if I wanted to. It was warm and soft. After that, I combed it every chance I got whenever I visited.

Then one day Mummy said she was taking me to visit Nennie because she was ill. A thorn had scratched her foot in her garden, and it had "turned bad." Nennie's "bad" foot persisted and each time I visited, the house smelled more of disinfectant and medicine. Faithful to the end, Nennie's old friend Miss Lou cared for her daily, making sure that she was clean, comfortable and fed. The doctor visited regularly, and Granny and Mummy took Dell and me on Sunday afternoons to sing choruses at Nennie's bedside when she was confined to bed.

I know that we were not the only visitors because over the period of Nennie's illness, the number of curio items and ornaments dwindled until eventually all that remained were the mahogany tables and shelves which Miss Lou continued to polish to a high shine, just as she continued to make sure that Nennie's room was cheerful, clean and aired. Finally, Mummy told me one afternoon, "Vaughna, your Nennie has gone to be with the Lord."

I cried. I took ill the day of the funeral and was unable to attend.

## *Chapter Two*

Seated at the dining table picking rice one Saturday night for Sunday lunch the next day, I heard my mother and grandmother talking about the new owners of Nennie's house. When they realized I was all ears, they made a lesson of it as they did with most issues.

"Nennie left the property to Miss Lou in her will, but three lawyers decided it was too good for her, so they managed to take it for themselves."

"Miss Lou quietly left them to it, but she said that none of them will benefit from it," Mummy interjected.

"Now you children are not too young to understand me. I want you when you grow up to do any honest job to earn a living. Any honest job. Just don't become a lawyer ... too much lying and thieving."

Seven weeks later, one of the three lawyers shot himself in the mouth in full view of the neighbours. On returning from work, he stepped out of his vehicle, took his licensed firearm from his briefcase and shot himself in the mouth, right in his front yard. Exactly seven weeks after that another of the lawyers fried to death when in a drunken stupor, he lost control of his vehicle which ran off the road and hit a utility pole. The live wires fell on the car and turned it into a sizzling saucepan. He was pronounced dead at the scene. The third lawyer left the country seven weeks later and has not been heard of since.

The village folk talked about these events in turn as they occurred, and then they observed as Miss Lou moved out of the house with just her small grip. She locked the mahogany front door and carried the keys to the Calliaqua Police Station on her way to moving in with her son. Marvin and his wife Petrina lived in the neighbouring village, Calliaqua. They had renovated their house by adding a one-bedroom apartment to accommodate Miss Lou so she could maintain her independence while not being alone. There, she was expected to live a long and happy life with her grandchildren around her. The village settled down once more to its daily routine.

The village, called Arnos Vale, was like many other villages and at the same time unlike any other. Gentle green hillsides protected the lower lying flatlands which accommodated our sole mainland airport, the E. T. Joshua Airport. Arnos Vale could alternately have been a seaport, being right on the southeastern coast. There was not much evidence of a well-planned settlement, but Arnos Vale managed to attach itself to a number of roadways that converged into one main highway leading to the city. Village life was close-knit since those who did not actually live on the flatlands were able to see what took place there from their vantage points on the slopes. Additionally, most residents knew each other by virtue of having lived there all their lives.

Arnos Vale sported its own crop of academics and professionals and could hold its own with the surrounding villages, Calliaqua, Belair and Belmont. It had its own school and airport as mentioned before, and the prestigious Arnos Vale Sports Complex, and by right should have been given the distinction of a town. Several churches dotted the landscape of Arnos Vale and just as many small business places sprang up almost overnight giving the uninitiated the impression that Arnos Vale was in fact a town.

Most of the residents of Arnos Vale who were not actually born there grew up there. The parents simply left their property to their children who were minded to remain in the village. Everybody knew everybody else and knew their ancestry too. I was too young to keep track of all our neighbours, but that experience with Nennie and her property made such an impression on me that it became second nature for me to observe keenly anyone with whom I came into contact. Although I wasn't sure exactly what I was looking for, I already had a clearly defined image of what honest people looked like and who could be classified as neighbour. Now I believe I was subconsciously seeking honesty and sincerity in the people I encountered. Very little escaped my little ears and eyes then.

Somewhere close to my eleventh birthday I had another encounter with a dog. I had gone to take a message to the neighbours whom we called Tanty and Pappy and who lived two houses away to our right. They owned two huge German Shepherds that looked to me as though they were the size of ponies. One was fat and the other was lean. As usual, I was wary of these beasts. They were customarily tied at their kennels and that was just the case when I arrived.

I knocked and gained entry to the kitchen and having delivered my message to Tanty, I took my leave.

When I exited the kitchen and stepped into the yard, I heard a low growl. I didn't see the dog, but I didn't need to. I had already cleared the field that was Tanty and Pappy's kitchen garden and I could hear the labouring breath of the fat Ritzie giving chase. I took the fence that separated that piece of land from our immediate neighbours' with the stride of a professional hurdler. The trip across the neighbours' front yard was accomplished in next to no time and I was on the home stretch, across the plot of land that was boundary to ours, past the flower garden and the guava tree and into the porch where I saw Mummy and Granny awaiting my return. Adrenalin pumping, I raced into the porch like an athlete making a final lunge at the finish line. Mummy jumped down from her seat on the porch wall to hold me still as I was uncontrollably running on the spot and gasping, "Ritzie! Ritzie!"

"Nobody... nothing is chasing you!" she shouted shaking me firmly into submission. With my legs finally at standstill, my shoulders and chest heaved as I fought for a calming breath.

After I had calmed down enough to drink some water and explain what had happened, Mummy walked over to Tanty's, using the road and learned that Pappy, thinking that I had already left, set Ritzie loose for her afternoon run. By the time he realized what was happening and called the dog, it immediately gave up the chase because I was no longer on the premises. Mummy returned home and warned me again about running from dogs.

"That's when they chase you," she explained patiently. "Pick up a stone or stick, but don't run." I heard her, but I wasn't sure I could comply.

Then just when I thought we had had our surfeit of dogs, at around the age of fifteen Dell visited another neighbour on a Girl Guide mission. When their Rottweiler came bounding up as Mrs. Hinds let her through the gate, Dell stood her ground. The dog lumbered up to her, sniffed her and sank its teeth into her left thigh - through her skirt and all. Visibly distressed, Mr. and Mrs. Hinds rushed her off to A&E where a Tetanus shot was administered, and the wound cleaned and dressed. When they brought Dell back home from the hospital and explained with much apologizing to Mummy and Granny what had happened, I started to ask her why she hadn't run and was immediately shushed.

Tenacious as a limpet, I awoke first next morning and with my fist supporting my jaw, I stared Dell into wakefulness. When I repeated my question, she presented two reasons that were good enough for me. Firstly, there was nowhere to run to and secondly, the dog was conniving. It pretended to be friendly then bit her. She didn't know it then, but she taught me two valuable lessons. You can't trust man's best friend, so you should be safe not trusting man himself; they could both be conniving. Secondly, you always have to have somewhere to run to.

## *Chapter Three*

It wasn't until I was well into my teenage years that I realized that I had been regularly carted off to the most unlikely places to keep me "out of mischief." Of course, no one thought I deserved an explanation of what mischief I was prone to attract, but sometime between my encounter with the Harrys' dog and Nennie's death Mummy took me to a funeral. I deduced, erroneously, I must admit, from conversation around me, that the deceased was the wife of a lawyer who lived on the other side of the village. I could not remember having seen her alive although I had walked past that house at least once a week. That alone should have alerted me to my mistake, but it didn't.

The house in question looked interesting from outside. It was the first building I had seen made from real river stones at the bottom and board at the top. A covered river-stone staircase led from outside to the upper floor which was the dwelling house. When the wind blew up the curtains, I could see through the window, a square clock flanked by two pictures on a partition, and sometimes I thought I saw the face of an old woman. Downstairs housed an organization of some sort, for the furniture there consisted of some benches and an enormous desk.

Inquisitively, I looked forward to the funeral and expected that I would see exactly what the inside of that house was like. The day of the funeral arrived and with it a brief period of disappointment, for instead of making our way to the other side of the village, Mummy took a bus to Kingstown.

"Yes, the funeral is in town," she had anticipated my question. We went to a two storey building in the capital, Kingstown. The front door really wasn't a front door but rather something of a wooden gate hanging on very large hinges. The gate opened onto what looked like a small courtyard. A stone staircase with newly painted reddish-brown pipe rails led upstairs on the outside to a landing and a door, and beneath the landing was a door which I imagined was the downstairs front door. We entered through that door and it took a while for my eyes to adjust to the gloom of the corridor after the bright sunlight outside. At the end of the surprisingly ample corridor, a woman in black and white ushered us towards a wooden staircase on her right and following the couple ahead of us, we climbed the stairs. A number of people were gathered in one corner of the fairly large room where an opened coffin occupied an almost central position. There was nothing cheerful about this room that I was forced to compare with Nennie's. Wherever there were curtains, they were severely drawn together. Chairs were pushed back against the partitions which bore framed pictures of Christ and His disciples at the Last Supper, and Christ ascending to heaven on a cloud as His followers gazed in awe. One partition was dedicated to three pictures of bowls of flowers arranged in step-like ascending order. Mummy followed the other mourners as they filed past the coffin to view the body and I headed for the one window that was wide open and through which a gusty breeze blew. The window opened onto one of the three streets in the city and I was supposedly engrossed in the activities immediately below me when I realized that I was also unintentionally eavesdropping on a conversation between two ladies located maybe two feet away from my right elbow.

"She looks really dark. I nearly didn't recognize her."

"Me too! But you know they say that's how they change colour when they are poisoned."

"Hmm…. You think that could really be true?"

"Well, it won't be the first time. They say the same thing happened to the first one."

"He can't be so brazen," the first speaker murmured.

"I am not putting it past him," was her companion's succinct observation.

Suddenly a short man in a black jacket bustled into the room.

"Close the coffin!" he commanded. His mouse-like features

looked nervously around the room where nobody moved.

"Where the pallbearers?" he demanded.

The mourners began filing down the staircase and I couldn't help but notice that the coffin was actually placed close to the curtained door that led to the outside staircase. I wondered why it wasn't opened.

The two ladies had started down the stairs ahead of me, and Mummy followed. We were almost to the bottom of the stairs when the lady in front cried, "Oh God!" and toppled down the rest of the stairs. Her friend hurried to her assistance. With help, she hobbled to a chair nearby and I saw that her stockings were torn and one of her considerably high heels broken. Mummy went over to see if she was all right and suggested that she be given some water to drink. I know that she would have stayed to help but I was tugging at her hand and whispering urgently to her to let's go. Aided by some men who had been milling about in the street below, the mouse-faced man was bringing the coffin downstairs to be placed in the hearse.

I needed to get away because I had convinced myself that the dead woman had somehow managed to trip that woman causing her to tumble down. I do not recall going to the church for the funeral service. What I do recall is that after the funeral, I could not eat for a few days. It was a good thing that all this had happened during the school vacation. For a whole week after that incident, I was listless and seemingly in a daze. I had to be bathed and dressed and fed like a baby. I spoke to no one. I did not seek food.

The ladies' conversation replayed itself in my subconsciousness and my imagination conjured up a face that was fair gradually turning darker. I was afraid to close my eyes. Mummy and Granny prayed over me every night to get me to sleep and asked the Lord to release me from the "melancholy fit" which had engulfed me. After nearly two weeks their prayers were finally answered. I told Mummy I didn't want to go to any funerals again.

My sudden and unexplained illness on the day of Nennie's funeral was sufficient reminder and elicited no comment.

## Chapter Four

Dell was really concerned about me. Of the two of us, she was the more reflective. When I confided in her about the jumbie pushing down the lady at the funeral she tried to convince me that firstly there was no such thing as a jumbie and secondly that dead people can't do things like pushing down live people.

"Unheard of!" she had dismissed.

I remained unconvinced and avoided all funerals thereafter. Then one afternoon we were returning from a church function when an ambulance screamed to a halt at the house with the river stone bottom. A little old lady was brought out on a stretcher and carried away in the ambulance. When we arrived home and relayed the information, Mummy seemed reluctant to comment except to remark, "Oh, old Mrs. Smith."

Well, I took a break from my homework to process that piece of information. Since she was old Mrs. Smith, then the lawyer whose wife had died had to be Mr. Smith. I had still not seen anyone else at that house, but I had other interesting things to occupy my time, so I dismissed the Smiths.

Not far along the same street with the Smiths there lived a really lovely lady by the name of Mrs. Lesline. I just liked to look at her. Having lived overseas for several years, she talked differently. Her gold-rimmed spectacles could not hide the merry glitter in her eyes. Her face was round and smooth, and her hair was thick, black, and long. She usually wore her hair in a thick roll at the nape of her neck and sported a variety of broad brimmed hats that I supposed were to shield her light brown complexion from our unrelenting tropical sun. Her large gold earrings added to the cheerfulness of her features and when she spoke or smiled, I was fascinated by the two gold teeth that flashed between her rouged lips. She fitted my impression of Enid Blyton's gypsies.

To us children in the village and those surrounding, she was a fairy godmother. Granny said she was a philanthropist. Her overseas visits were now confined to the six warmer months of the year, spending the colder months here at home and doing so in style. Every New Year's Day she organized a picnic for us children. Food and drink were plentiful and to spare. Even after being fed, each child was presented with a party bag full of goodies to take home. That was in addition to the gift and sometimes gifts that each child received. Everyone looked forward to the picnic, usually held at the beach, and talked about it long afterwards. Parents were encouraged to come with their children and assist with the supervision of the sea bathing.

These picnics were always well attended. It was to her credit that the picnics were so well coordinated that over the years, never was there an accident. Her children, nieces and nephews assisted in some preparation of the food and the rest was catered. The gifts consisted of toys as well as items for school.

Apart from this general act of generosity, Mrs. Lesline was known for meeting the needs of the less fortunate in the village. She was also a known disciplinarian. One afternoon, she seemed to be just returning home as a couple of us approached her house. When she looked up after fastening the latch on her white wooden gate, we called out the mandatory courteous, "Good afternoon, Mrs. Lesline," and were alarmed when we heard a sharp, "Good afternoon," and then, "Come here, little one." Mrs. Lesline was wearing a simple but elegant flowered aquamarine and white dress with a belt of the same colour at the waist. On her feet were a pair of royal blue shoes with the cutest little heels and on her head was the ever-present hat with a white band. Adjusting her royal blue tote bag securely on her left forearm, she had singled out Tedica with a glittering stare, so we pushed her forward.

"What happened to your shoes?" Mrs. Lesline inquired gently.

"They mash up," Tedica mumbled.

"Speak up now," she commanded eyeing the offending shoes

with the condemnation they deserved. "Who is your mother?"

"Mamee," replied a nervous Tedica and earned herself a nudge from one of us.

"Diana John, Mrs. Lesline," I volunteered.

"Well, what is your name and where do you live?" Mrs. Lesline persisted. "Good clear English, mind you," she added.

Tedica hesitated and then put her best foot forward. "My name is Tedica John and I live up the road and then across the road in Arnos Vale, Mrs. Lesline."

"Okay then, Tedica, hurry home now and tell your mother to come and see me." We took off up the road and although I was not in place to accurately recount the encounter, I know it was productive because next Monday morning Tedica was wearing a brand new pair of school shoes and socks in which she stepped very carefully.

Next New Year's Day picnic, several pairs of shoes were among the gifts that were distributed. We lined up in an orderly fashion and were each given a pair of black socks. The couple that was in charge of the shoe distribution subjected our feet to measured scrutiny then selected the estimated size from the boxes stacked in the covered back of a vehicle. More often than not, the shoes turned out to be the right fit when tried with the socks. We also received a backpack each. Where the need was most urgent the school bags were immediately pressed into service when school reopened. Mummy made us put up ours for the new school year.

Then one Saturday morning Dell and I were walking down the road when she grabbed my hand and pulled me to a halt.

"Watch!" was all she managed. My jaw dropped. A Bulldozer was razing the Smiths' house! I stood there trembling uncontrollably. We watched in stunned silence, then when we were able, by tacit agreement we crossed the road and continued to the shop on the corner.

We hurried back home barely talking, but as soon as we entered the house we began in unison.

"They are breaking down the Smiths' house!"

"Well, that is only to be expected," was Granny's cryptic response.

"You knew?" Dell and I queried almost in unison again. We got no response and knew better than to pursue the issue, but the weight of each load of rubble from that building seemed to have been deposited on us.

Even so, life had to go on, so having saved a small fortune selling fudge in school at break time and at home on afternoons, I presented myself at a bank in town to open a savings account and make my grand deposit. Like those before me I joined the queue that snaked from the door to the tellers. I was at the last curve in the line with a clear view of the other end of the bank over which hung signs that read, "Customer Service," "Foreign Drafts" and "Loans," when in bustled the short mouse-faced undertaker wearing a jacket that flapped open in front him. He pushed past the clients at Customer Service and moved to the front of the Foreign Drafts queue beside the person who had the attention of the clerk.

"I want a draft for ten thousand dollars U.S." he declared. The clerk barely noticed him as a murmur went up from the clients.

The lady in front of me muttered, "His mother, poor Mrs. Smith, must be rolling over in her grave." Mouse face turned impatiently to a disgruntled-looking young man, also dressed in a black suit and who had followed him up to the counter.

"I have to get this now. Let's go!" So saying, he wheeled and stomped out of the bank.

"Who he think he is?" somebody near me asked. Comments flew like sharp darts in all directions.

Once more I was stunned. That odious man was actually Mr. Smith the lawyer. He was not the undertaker that I had presumed him to be at the funeral! I gathered from the talk swirling around me that that man had it coming to him.

"What ain't meet him ain't pass him!" was one dark observation.

Ascribed to him was the dastardly act of taking his mother to his home upon her discharge from hospital. There he claimed that she signed a document leaving the property to him. She died shortly after. He had three other siblings. When they protested, he razed the house and transferred the property to his son's name. The siblings did not want to sully the name of the Smiths so they left him alone. As soon as the dust had settled, he sold the property and pocketed the money.

When I returned home, I shared the information with Mummy and Granny and from their reaction, they must have been aware of the murky details of Mr. Smith's life. Granny looked over the rim of her spectacles and issued a reminder.

"Remember what I told you about any honest job? Apparently it is very easy for people of that profession to become dishonest."

## *Chapter Five*

School life became all-consuming and what was left was dedicated to church. School meant excelling academically and at the chosen extra-curricular activities. There was no other option. Ironically, despite my penchant for taking to my heels at a mere suggestion of danger, Dell was the one who excelled at track and field and netball. I took on volleyball and netball.

Church was a meaningful experience. There was Sunday School and singing in the junior choir and saying of recitations at Harvest. Harvest was the high point of church activities for the year. Decorating the church for the event kept us occupied late into Saturday night and it was always a joy to view the finished product. Cane stalks framed the doorways and on Harvest Sunday, the tables were arrayed with every imaginable fruit or homemade delectable ranging from fudge to cupcakes, lime balls, ginger sticks, sugar cakes of all kinds and colours, jams and jellies of all descriptions; guava cheese; drinks of all fruits.

The major attraction was the money tree. I was never sure how that particular enterprise worked, but by all accounts, it realized a huge profit on a yearly basis until a learned Reverend decreed that that practice was akin to merchandizing for which Christ had chastised the money changers in Matthew 21:12 -13, Mark 11:15 – 17 and John 12:14 – 16. The money tree never appeared again at Harvest and inexplicably, Harvest lost its appeal thereafter.

By this time, I had honed my observation skills and realized that church held too many distractions away from the sermon. I decided that I would go to church with Granny instead of with most of my village friends.

At the same time of my switching churches there was one enormous wedding in the village. The announcement caused a stir because when it became public knowledge, it was accompanied by the statement that the only virgin in Arnos Vale was getting married. I knew the young lady in question, and she had every right to be a virgin. I had no problem with that. I just couldn't help wondering firstly how it came about that everyone seemed to be in possession of this information and secondly who had examined the rest of us to have us relegated to less than virgins. Granny and Mummy had received an announcement, but since that was not an invitation, it really did not fall into the category of "Featured Event" for us. However, as fate would have it, Dell and I had loitered too long at a new variety store on the other side of the village and were attempting to get home by means of a short cut when we found our path blocked by people and vehicles. Then we remembered the happy event. The crowd in the church yard was so thick that the vehicle bringing the bride-to-be encountered great difficulty manoeuvring to the church entrance. Dell and I were not so hampered. We wormed our way through the crush, careful to mutter, "Excuse me please," (just in case someone complained to Mummy and Granny) until we arrived at the wall enclosing the church yard. With ease of habit, we climbed up and sat upon the wall from which vantage point we had an unimpeded view of the church door. The yard itself was crowded with spectators jostling for the best view.

From the bridal car stepped the maid of honour, Phillippa Mason. She looked pretty in a pink dress that reminded me of icing on a cake. Then she turned to assist the bride-to-be. Andrina seemed to appear from the car in degrees - feet in dainty silver shoes with filigree bows at the front; then her head on which was a fluffy veil attached to a silver tiara; then appeared an equally fluffy Andrina followed by cumulative rising murmurs of the spectators. Dell and I nearly fell from our privileged perch as Andrina, face unveiled and beautiful as ever flashed a happy smile in the direction of the crowd and proceeded into the church on her brother's arm to be united with her groom. Already late, we waited where we were until the ceremony over, Andrina and her Phillip came beaming down the aisle and outside to the awe-hushed villagers. The newly-weds took their seats in a white convertible, hired and decorated for the occasion, and followed by the guests, with much horn blowing, were driven to the venue for the reception.

We jumped off the wall and hurried home knowing full well we were in trouble. The parents were waiting for us as we hesitantly approached the door.

"I wonder where you two young ladies are coming from at this time?" Granny started.

"And you had better speak the truth because you know we would find out," Mummy warned.

"We stayed to look at the wedding," Dell confessed.

"And Andrina looked really pretty and happy, but she's not a virgin because she's pregnant," I reported. Before I had a chance to escape, Mummy had me by my lower lip.

"How many times must I tell you not to repeat everything you hear?" she demanded pinching hard. When she released me, I muttered, "We saw her pregnant. She's not a virgin!"

"Vaughna!" Mummy warned.

Hurt and hungry, I slunk to the kitchen in search of food. Dell nudged me out of the way at the fridge door and quickly organized a snack for both of us. When we were seated at the table she mused, "I wonder how that rumour got started. Sounds like not everything we hear is true."

"Well," I said through a mouth full of food, "she was a virgin before she got pregnant anyway."

## Chapter Six

Hardly had that wave of excitement settled to a ripple when the village was abuzz once more. The Samuel family lived on the other side of the village in a relative's house which they were renting. Mr. Samuel was an Accountant by profession and the church Treasurer and Mrs. Samuel was a nurse. Tessa Samuel and I were around the same age and had been friends for years. We were sure that her older brother Steven had his eyes on Dell, and we kept our eyes on them as much as we could so we could exchange notes. Since we were now part of the young people's group of the church, we were always involved in the activities. One day towards the end of February, Tessa informed me that their papers for migration to the United States of America had "come through" and they were planning to leave by Easter – in a month's time. I was devastated. When I walked into our room one afternoon and found Dell sitting at the foot of the bed and hurriedly trying to put away a photo of Steven, I couldn't even relay the information to Tessa. The days sped by and the reality of the Samuels' departure was confirmed when they were given the customary send off at church. They were surrounded by a circle of fellowship and wished well and prayed for that Sunday.

When Tuesday morning arrived, I was at the airport along with a few well-wishers to see the family off. Tessa and I hugged and promised to keep in touch. Dell and Steven kept their distance until the very last minute. Then they hugged, and he disappeared into the Departure Lounge.

Two weeks later while in a minivan to school I realized that the Samuels were the topic of a conversation between the lady in the corner beside me and one in the row in front her, also in the corner.

"Cleaned out the church account and bale out with his whole family!" the one beside me declared.

"So I hear, but that can't be true. He wasn't working?" The lady in front was turned sideways, the better to keep up with the conversation.

"What that have to do with anything? The church people trying to hush it up, but you know that sort of thing can't stay cover down," the first speaker opined.

There was no doubt in my mind that there was some horrible truth to the conversation. My head spun and my palms began sweating. How positively terrible! When I came off the bus without hearing any more of the conversation because I had arrived at my bus stop, I could hardly see where I was going. The day dragged by – a most horrible seven hours.

"What's bothering you now?" Mummy challenged as I tried without success to swallow my food that afternoon. "You have mail from Tessa," she said sliding an air mail envelope bearing Tessa's handwriting to me. I tore the envelope and read:

*Hi Vaughna,*

*By now you must have heard the story. Don't think badly of us. Daddy had left a letter explaining his actions. He has since written to the church and made arrangements to repay the money that he borrowed. We didn't have enough funds to cover our travel and settling in expenses and Daddy really didn't know what again to do since we didn't have collateral to get a regular loan. We have all started working and Daddy estimates that we should be able to repay the twenty thousand ($20,000) dollars with interest by the end of the year. As you can see, we live in Philly and our apartment is not far from school. Steven works at a Duane Reade about four blocks away, three evenings a week and weekends, and I got into KMart where I am signed up for a minimum of thirty six (36) hours per week. It's been going good so far. Daddy got a position with a private accounting firm and Mummy had no problem settling* *in at a hospital in a nearby County. Daddy said that with God's grace we would get ourselves sorted out and out of debt by end of year and then we would start saving to buy our own home, not necessarily here in Philly, but that is in the future. We would keep in touch so you could plan to come and visit. Be sure to keep me abreast of all the activities at home.*

*Love yah,*
*Tessa*

Mummy said, "I am happy for them."

My spirits lifted considerably, and I immediately started planning my response. "Just this morning two women were talking on the van and saying that Mr. Samuel emptied church account. I'm glad that's not true."

"What he did certainly wasn't right, but he has put things in place for restitution so we can't condemn him," Mummy said consolingly. "And remember what I have always told you about repeating everything you hear."

"I know," I smiled happily.

In June, Andrina and her Phillip became the proud parents of twin babies Arianne and Adrian.

## *Chapter Seven*

In September of that year, having been successful at her 'A' Levels, Dell found employment with an accounting establishment in the city and left me languishing in fifth form. I did not look forward to that school year with any enthusiasm, but since I had no choice in the matter, I went to school daily and persevered at all ten subjects which I was expected to pass at 'O' Level in May/June of the next year. I faced the prospect with the grimness of a woman in labour. By November, I was about to give up. I could see Granny and Mummy hovering, making sure that I put in extra hours of study. They had done the same for Dell and their efforts had paid off all the way to 'A' Levels.

In November, I received another letter from Tessa. By sacrifice and penny-pinching, they had repaid their debt and had begun saving towards a down payment for their own home. For some reason, that information spurred me on, and I became more diligent in my studies. Christmas holidays found me slaving at Maths, my worst subject. Dell stayed up with me some nights and helped me out. Then the arrival of Tessa's Christmas letter caused consternation in our household.

Shortly after the Samuels had left for the U.S.A. another family moved into the house they had vacated. It was a family of five – a girl who was working in town, a boy in fourth form at a school in town, a child who looked about eight and the parents who were civil servants. We classified the man as old and his wife as around Mummy's age. It turned out that they were the Dunbars who had started constructing a monstrosity of a building at the northwestern end of the village. The land was just under a hill close to which ran one of the two rivers that passed through the village to the sea. I recalled hearing that decades ago piece of the mountain side had slipped into the river in bad weather and had formed the piece of land which had very slightly changed the original course of the river. That plot of land was therefore considered a 'reserve' and from time to time ambitious villagers had planted flowers and maintained the area as a beauty spot, so wedding parties often had their photographs taken there. The affected villagers were peeved when the land was suddenly annexed and construction began there, because it was obvious to all that Mr. Dunbar had used his political connections to secure the land. Bearing in mind its size, it was impossible for this construction to escape the notice of any villager, but since it was outside our usual route of travel, its presence did not unduly affect us. What was however noticeable was that the concrete walls had darkened over time and some of the bamboo scaffolding had succumbed to weathering. To us children, it was just a house that was unfinished. However, to the villagers, the Dunbars had several strikes against them.

Firstly, they were not originally from Arnos Vale. They had no relatives there. Secondly, they had appropriated for their personal use, land that was allocated for the use of the entire village and thirdly they obviously couldn't finish the house. Naturally, the villagers set about finding out all they could about these interlopers.

The house newly occupied by the Dunbars was owned by Tessa's Great Aunt Melanie. She had inherited it from her parents and when she married Hubert Marshall, they lived in the house until they migrated about twenty years ago. At that time, they had left in place an arrangement for Lawyer Smith to oversee and rent the house and take care of necessary repairs, all for a fee. That arrangement obtained when the Samuels rented and occupied the property.

Well, according to Tessa, about a month after they arrived in Philly, Great Aunt Melanie asked her Dad about the arrears of the rent. Mr. Samuel had no idea what she was talking about. The discussion that ensued led to her Dad producing a number of receipts for the years they had occupied the house. He was making regular three months' advance payments. Where he didn't have receipts, he got bank records showing regular payments going to the Smith and Smith law firm. After that, everything began unraveling.

Great Aunt Melanie contacted Lawyer Smith and asked him to settle the account for the house. He had responded that he was involved in a demanding lawsuit at the time and promised to contact her as soon as the matter was concluded. He had further added that since the Samuels left he had rented the property. That correspondence was in June.

"Quite June!" Mummy interrupted. "This is December!"

"So they have decided to sell the house," I informed them, quickly reading further in the letter. "They say that taking into consideration health care and everything else, they are better off where they are in the States."

Granny shook her head and tut tutted. "I don't know what this world is coming to when people just can't be trusted!"

I finished reading the letter and started getting ready to respond.

A few days later we heard that there was to be no New Year's picnic because Mrs. Lesline had fallen ill.

Christmas was quiet as usual. Dell got us all really neat presents. I got a stackable tray in which I could store all my hair products. I got her a new makeup compact. She had been scraping the bottom crevices of hers for weeks. Granny got a new pair of church shoes and Mummy got a voucher for a pedicure at a reputable establishment. She was pleased but she wanted to know what was wrong with her soaking her feet in Epsom salts and warm water.

As usual, midnight Old Year's Night found us praying in the New Year. "Watchnight" service was held at church at ten o'clock until midnight to New Year's morning, but Granny preferred us to be at home in prayer, at the beginning of the new year. She reminded us that the New Year is a leap year and that the devil is most voracious in a leap year. She prayed fervently for us, for our friends, relatives, the government and opposition, people in authority, police, lawyers and judges, doctors, nurses, teachers and school children, workers and business people. I must have started to snore because Dell poked me alert hissing sharply, "Girl!" I feigned attention and hurried off to my bed as soon as the final "Amen!" sounded.

## *Chapter Eight*

Granny must have had a prophetic epiphany because January had barely begun when there was talk about elections that year.

When trading of political accusations began, an editorial in one of the local weekly newspapers was out front declaring that "corruption was endemic in government as well as in the society." In the brief editorial, the Editor cited seven incidents in support of his claim. One of them had to do with the electoral list and the population census. I had to wonder whether I had dreamt seeing boxes marked CENSUS and a group of young people in a government office diligently rubbing out information from documents. I had misread washroom directions and wandered into the office where the door seemed to have been inadvertently left ajar. Unable to separate fantasy from reality, I remained silent.

In the political fray, the ruling Revolutionary Labour Party (RLP) was accused of "blatant disregard for the tenets of democracy" and "alienating themselves from the truth." In turn, they charged that the opposition Conservative Democratic Party (CDP) was "weak" and that its leader "waffled on critical issues." A third party known as the Party for Social Preservation

(PSP) had been vigorously and unrelentingly criticizing the policies of the government since last elections. And then, completely ignoring the view that two's company and three's a crowd, there arose another entity that declared itself not to be a political party. It joined the political wrangling under the name of the Progressive Movement for Social Unity (PMSU).

I nearly fell off the porch wall one night when the strident voice of the Prime Minister reached us from the other side of the village. "If the Conservative Democratic Party win this election, God Bible write wrong!"

Granny declared that that was the worst piece of blasphemy she had heard in her life. The next morning's news reported that the Prime Minister's doctor had advised him to rest for a week or so as he had sustained injuries to his leg and ankle the night before. Apparently while descending from the platform, he had fallen down the few makeshift steps. Granny murmured, "Lord Jesus, help us!"

I remembered Mrs. Smith's funeral and shuddered.

My Social Studies School Based Assessment (SBA) on the effects of partisan politics on my community evolved into a profound revelation of the filth of politics. I managed to collect the data for the project only because I was canvassing my community in which almost everyone knew me. Apart from gathering the data for my study, I engaged my respondents in discussion on issues that formed the basis for the word-slinging between the two leading parties. It was in one such discussion that I obtained much information about the Dunbars. Mr. Dunbar had come to the village with hands that were decidedly dirty.

He had his origins on the leeward side of the island and had joined the teaching profession with minimum entry level qualifications shortly after leaving secondary school. According to my informant, "At the end of that school year his name and that of a female student were mentioned in the same sentence, so during the long holidays, he disappeared." Thereafter his checkered past seemed to have eluded the young lady who eventually became his wife, or Cupid's most potent arrow must have struck her at the most vulnerable period of her life. Granny and Mummy would have fixed me with a censoring glare had they been aware of my interest, but that was no deterrent to my asking one respondent how she knew so much about the family. The master of the household stated frankly that when a newcomer started a house so long ago and appeared not to be able to finish it, there was need for inquiry. I pondered all I had heard and then made a valiant effort to shelve that topic in preference to my studies.

## *Chapter Nine*

Dawn broke grey and somber on the first Tuesday in February. There was an unnatural hush around the village and villagers moved with seeming reluctance. Mrs. Lesline had passed away in the early hours of the morning. Villagers, soberly dressed, conversed in muted tones and mourned. Tributes to Mrs. Lesline poured out from every door. Not an ill word was spoken about her. The village lay in mourning until her funeral a week later. Friends and relatives from all over the world came to pay their final respects. Granny and Mummy said that the church was packed, with people standing against the walls on all sides, even around the choir platform. Mourners filled the church yard and spilled out onto the street. Every adult male who had benefitted from Mrs. Lesline's kindness wanted a chance to bear her simple wooden coffin from the church to the hearse. Granny declared that she had never seen anything like it before. Singing and clapping, the cortege consisting of several buses hired for the event and even more private vehicles made its way to the cemetery in the next village where Mrs. Lesline was lovingly laid to rest. A cool mist hovered over the entire proceedings.

Very slowly, life in Arnos Vale returned to normal. Like other school children, I went to school and studied. Dell, like others, went to work. We went to church, to Young Peoples' meetings, tried to keep abreast of the fashion trends and to stay slim like the Hollywood stars.

Then Tessa responded to my letter. Great Aunt Melanie and Great Uncle Hubert were coming home to see about settling the account with Lawyer Smith and finalizing the sale of the property. I wrote back giving her an update of the school sports meet and the Firms' Netball Competition in which Dell was her firm's Goal Shoot. By the time I was finished jumping up and down and cheering her along, I was as tired as if I had been playing the game myself. I had completed my SBAs, and revision was the order of the day for most classes as the syllabuses had been completed. I stuck gamefully to my study timetable.

Dell's firm was expanding, and since she seemed to have natural Mathematical acumen, they had offered her the opportunity to pursue actuarial studies. They would provide 80% financing and one year's full pay and she would be contracted to return to work with them. That meant going to England to pursue studies in Actuarial Science. I didn't want to think about that so I avoided the subject as far as I could.

A month to the day of Mrs. Lesline's funeral, Mr. Lesline, her husband of fifty-seven years slipped away to meet her in the life hereafter. He too was given a rousing send off by the villagers. He was buried beside his wife.

Politically, "acrimony," seemed to be the buzzword. Reckless pronouncements were attributed to the governing RLP every day. The electorate was more severely divided with ardent followers swearing to go with the Prime Minister wherever he leads them. Evidence of the crumbling infrastructure of the country left the discerning citizen speechless. In reality, the nation was enduring a season of dissatisfaction with a government which appeared to be living in a gold lined insulated bubble, far removed from the lives of the majority of the population.

Easter came and so did Tessa's response. Great Aunt Melanie and Great Uncle Hubert returned to the USA without having had the opportunity to see Lawyer Smith. On each occasion that they arranged to meet with him, he was unavoidably detained elsewhere. When they decided to stake out his office, taking turns to ensure that one of them was always there, he never appeared for the entire day! The property had been sold to a gentleman living in the British Virgin Islands (BVI) who was aware of the circumstances surrounding the occupation of the house.

He claimed he was not quite ready to take possession of the dwelling house but was tying up some business matters in the BVI before coming home. Meanwhile, he had given the Dunbars notice.

Granny said, "Could it be that these people don't read their Bibles?" That night I again heard her fervently petitioning divine intervention in this leap year. She pleaded that a shield be placed around the nation.

## *Chapter Ten*

The end of June arrived and having completed my CSEC O' Levels, I was officially on vacation. I took to making sure that I covered my chores and some of Dell's on a daily basis to make up for having been relieved of my responsibilities thereby allowing me to adequately prepare for my exams. After that, a group of us who had studied together took regular trips to the beach.

Granny got hold of us one morning when four of my friends were helping me with a chore. I had removed and washed the cushion covers the day before and we were putting them back on. When she heard that we had planned to go to the beach, Granny wanted to know if we couldn't find a better way to occupy ourselves.

"Sea water doesn't have back door," she cautioned.

Mummy wasn't comfortable and warned us to be careful.

"I don't like the dream I had last night," she said, grave concern evident in her voice and on her face. "Be careful."

We promised to exercise extreme caution and were soon on our way before they completely refused to let us go. As it was already past mid-morning, we decided to travel by van rather than take the twenty-minute walk. The route involved passing over a small bridge. Just before meeting the bridge, a road turned off on the left. A huge building was under construction at this juncture, and the project was temporarily enclosed as was required by law.

As the van in which we were travelling approached the bridge, a SUV coming from the opposite direction sped off the bridge and into a right turn directly in the path of the van. The van driver immediately applied his brake. Failing to properly make the turn, the SUV and its driver careened through the barricade around the construction and crashed into the building. Swearing, the van driver continued on his way.

"You see that! If I didn't stop I woulda hit him and it woulda look like if I wrong when is he who cut cross in front me!" the van driver complained.

We, the passengers were all in agreement. The five of us wanted to stop and go back but one of the passengers said it was just Mr. Smith and maybe he was just getting what he had coming to him. I wondered if that was Mummy's dream. I mused that it was really unfortunate that no one seemed to care that the poor man might be hurt.

The incident so reduced our enthusiasm for the beach that we curtailed our stay and began walking back home an hour later. When we arrived at the scene of the accident, the wrecked vehicle was being hoisted by the wrench of the tow truck. Among the spectators at the scene were some boys from the neighbourhood who, like us, were unoccupied having completed their exams. They admitted that it was just a matter of time before that accident happened.

"Is a habit the man have," Dave stated. "Whenever he coming off the bridge he don't wait on the traffic."

"We have been on the bridge and seen him do that same thing over and over," Rodney put in.

I asked, "Was he badly injured?"

Richie responded, "Well you see the condition of the ride. They had to cut him out of it."

We told them that we were in the van that avoided the collision.

"We had just come out on the bridge to chill as usual," gentleman Rodney continued. "Good thing you girls didn't stop. Smith cursed all the expletives we know and some new ones!"

"The man never even say, 'Lord have mercy', just a whole set ah bad words until it look like he faint," Dave recounted.

"Boy, I never see nor hear anything like that in my whole life!" Richie marveled.

"Watch how the man gone and dirty up the man wall just so and it ain't even paint yet!" a disgruntled construction worker growled fiercely behind me. Now that the vehicle had been pried away from the structure, he was inspecting the affected wall with undisguised malevolence.

We lingered another five minutes or so chatting with the boys and then headed home.

Although Granny and Mummy had heard about the accident, we told them what we had witnessed. I was disturbed that no one seemed too concerned about Smith's condition.

"Well, I guess we will hear of it on the TV news tonight," Granny predicted.

"Oh yes, the TV people were there when we passed," Natalia said.

"For all you know we might be on TV too," DeDe grinned. "I clean forgot I had seen them there."

After showering, we lazed around in my room and shortly after four o'clock DeDe and Natalia headed in one direction and Avril and Lenora headed for town.

The TV broadcast that night featured footage of the vehicle almost clamped to the wall and the newscaster said that Mr. Smith's condition was critical. Next morning the news was that Mr. Smith had been airlifted to the Q.E.H. in Barbados.

## *Chapter Eleven*

The days just before the release of our CSEC results, took a ride on the back of a limping tortoise. A group of young girls could enjoy going to the beach for so long and window shopping for so long, so those activities eventually began to pale. I wanted to offer to take care of the twins for Andrina and Phillip but Granny advised me to use the time to read my Bible. She suggested the book of John. I wasn't particularly enthused because I had been reading a variety of novels, among them Austin Clarke's *The Polished Hoe* and Charlotte Brontë's *Jane Eyre*, but the suggestion sounded more of a challenge to me, so I delved in.

Reading the Bible was nothing new for me, but that dedicated reading exercise proved to me, a revelation. I was firstly impressed by the language, and since my Bible had the words of Christ in red, I was able to pinpoint a number of interesting features. John introduced Jesus and was emphatic that His place was one of honour while John himself was merely to clear a path for Him. I looked at the metaphorical language in which Jesus claimed to be the bread of life, the door, the good shepherd and the true vine and showed how this is so. The book of John gives a vivid description of Jesus Christ and what His basic teachings are.

I was so impressed that I started to read from Matthew intending to read all of the New Testament. Then one day I happened on 2 Kings 7 in the Old Testament. After reading the entire chapter and allowing my imagination to run free on the events described there, I concluded that the Bible was a really interesting book. I was reading both New and Old Testaments when I realized that I was included in the "whosoever" of John 3:16. I admitted my need of salvation and believed. After hustling off a letter to Tessa that week, that Sunday I made my decision public in church.

Granny gave me a long lecture on what was expected of me as a Christian. Dell confessed that she had been struggling with a conviction for a while and then she too made her decision public and was subjected to a similar lecture. Now our church activities became more meaningful and we still had fun in our youth group.

The end of August finally arrived and news that CSEC results were out had us rushing excitedly but anxiously to school to await the release. Arriving nervously at the school office, I signed where the secretary expressionlessly indicated I should and was handed my result slip. By now my heart was throbbing in my throat. I shut my eyes, folded the slip and made my way downstairs to the yard. There, with trembling fingers I unfolded the slip ___ upside down! I righted it and scanned the right hand column. Nine ones and a two . . . for Maths! I realized I had been holding my breath when my vision blurred and I had to gasp for air. Then I was on a trampoline shouting, "Yes! Yes! Yes!" Then I breathed, "Thank you, Lord!"

I joined a group of fellow students where Avril and Lenora were clutching their results and refusing to open them. Natalia and DeDe were cajoling them with the encouragement that we had all passed. They finally opened them and then began a set of hugging and jumping up and yelling on the lawn that for all of our school life had been strictly out of bounds. We planned a celebration get-together. First, we headed for Dell's workplace, shared the good news and collected celebration funds, then called home. Granny and Mummy congratulated us and of course Granny had to warn me to conduct myself with decorum.

Since the popular fast-food restaurants were packed with other excited celebrating students and everyone seemed to be talking at the tops of their lungs, we decided to decentralize and settle for the largest waffle cones we could find. Then began our selection of courses for 'A' Level studies.

At home Granny and Mummy pored over the result slip and told me how pleased they were with my performance. I was especially happy that I had not disappointed them. We discussed my choice of courses, steering clear of anything mathematical.

That night I wrote Tessa a long letter.

## *Chapter Twelve*

The village appeared to have settled into a season of quiet reflection as the beginning of the new school year approached. There were still political engagements and the Prime Minister and his RLP gave the impression that they were confident of the majority support of the population. However, the Opposition activists were boring holes in their every proposition and effectively nullifying the propaganda which reached the public. There were a number of issues on which the CDP single-mindedly focused – corruption, education and health. For me, that was just a passing interest although I did accompany Dell when she went to register for her national ID card so she could vote for the very first time. I had school uniforms and books to think about. What I didn't want to think about was the likelihood that Dell would leave for England in early January.

Upon completing the registration process, I bought the fabric for the Community College uniform and Mummy set to work. I was measured, Mummy cut, and I offered to help with the basting. Then came the shirt-buying expedition. The group of us girls split up and searched every store in the city for just the right shirt then compared prices over waffle cones. We had just decided where we would shop when Agnes and Phyllis appeared, all excited.

"You got your tops already?" Phyllis queried. They didn't wait for a response.

"We got, out by a lady right in Arnos Vale. Shouldn't be too far from where you live, Vaughna," Agnes added.

"Oh? Who is that?"

"A Miss Payne, in that road leading to that big house that's not finished."

"Can't say I know that person," I worried, gnawing on my cone.

"She brings in all sorts of things to sell."

"Oh! Okay. I know who!" I conceded. "So let's see."

Phyllis produced a top for our inspection and it was agreed that Miss Payne's was the place for our tops. We would go visit her the next day.

Next day, when we turned off the main road and on to the village road on which Miss Payne lived, we encountered a commotion of enormous proportions. Some villagers had already gathered in the road outside the Dunbars' property. Others were hurrying up the road, passing us in their haste. Now, Dell and I had heard enough warnings about avoiding noisy crowds.

"Run away from confusion," Granny had warned time and again. I mentally justified our continued approach to Miss Payne's house with the rationale that we were on a mission and in no way were we joining the crowd. We didn't have to. From Miss Payne's yard we saw and heard enough.

In the shade of the grey and black mossy structure that looked like my impression of an old woman whose "grinders are few" (Ecclesiastes 12:3) a government registered truck was parked. The driver remained in his seat while the labourers doggedly offloaded lumber and cement and carried them into the unfinished structure. Creepers like matted hair clung to the side of the walls, almost to the top.

The villagers were incensed.

"Bold as brass!" one declared.

"Government material! Corruption!" another shouted.

"Waaa! Waaa! When yuh teefing, teef big!"

The cell phones and cameras were busy. The truck and number plates, perspiring workers, the building, and the very vocal crowd --- everything was immortalized. I was speechless. And as if that were not enough, another truck appeared. Well, it didn't quite reach the site. The crowd of onlookers parted temporarily as the truck veered to the left to make the turn on to the property. They came together again around the back half of the truck and with a protracted protesting hissing, dejectedly, the laden truck wobbled to a halt. All four back tyres were useless. The driver jumped out, surveyed the situation, and shook his head. He seemed to have arrived at a conclusion that was appropriate and favourable to the villagers, because when he locked the cab and walked back down the road, he did so to loud cheers, hoots and earsplitting whistles of approval. The two labourers jumped from the back of the vehicle and followed the driver at a short distance, looking back at the truck once in a while. I don't think my friends appreciated the significance of that incident, and we had other matters that claimed our attention, so we turned to the business at hand.

Miss Payne was a retired head teacher and operated her little boutique from an extension to her cottage. The addition was constructed to enhance the story-book-like appearance of her home. Gerberas, bougainvilleas and roses rioted in their semi-circular plots under her windows through which gaily coloured curtains fluttered. The 'Boutique' was set out for easy access to the variety of garments on display. In another section were samples of other items available. We selected our shirts, browsed around for a while and by noon we were ready to pay for our purchases and go home to model.

When we came out on the road, the disabled truck was right in the spot we had last seen it, but it was not exactly *how* we had last seen it. Yes, the tyres were still useless but the truck was also quite empty.

The villagers had helped themselves to everything on the truck. In all of this, the Dunbars never appeared. Apparently, no police report was made about the materials or the truck because nothing official was ever heard about the incident. I recounted the whole event to Dell who seemed quite put out at missing all the action since she was working.

## *Chapter Thirteen*

Dell couldn't complain next Saturday when she was right on the spot to see someone else the object of Mummy's ire. We were just about to attack the second half of our Saturday chores when a knocking was heard at the front door.

"Miss Craigg! Miss Craigg! Miss Toppin say to run come there quick. It urgent!" a young voice shouted.

Mummy looked out and inquired, "What?"

The youngster repeated the message and Mummy said, "All right," and hustled back inside to put on her outside shoes and hurry down the road. We were hard on her heels when she turned and sternly instructed, "Go right back!" Crestfallen, we slunk back into the house to complete our chores.

When she did return several hours later, Mummy was furious. We hesitated to ask why. She marched into the house and marched right out again and then stormed, "I don't know what she expected me to do!"

We waited in silence. "And this is none of your business, so don't let me hear you talk about it!"

Dell and I exchanged mystified glances. How could we talk about something we didn't know about? Curiosity nearly killed us. By the time Granny came back from spending the day with a relative who was returning to England the next day, Mummy had returned home and was calm enough to hold a civil conversation.

We learned that Mummy's friend Miss Toppin had undertaken to bake the black cakes for a wedding for a lady from the countryside. She had baked several cakes to make a huge display and the cakes had come out hard. Hard black cakes! So Miss Toppin called my mother to ask her what she could do to cause the cakes to revert to their batter consistency. That really annoyed Mummy. Where had one ever heard of anything so ridiculous? Mummy had set them to work blending new fruit and adding them to a mixture of strong rum and wine. Then she had started the baking process from scratch. That's what had taken her so long. The customer was collecting the cakes the next day to take them to the person who was doing the decorating. Mummy felt justifiably peeved.

"If she knew she couldn't bake black cake why didn't she just say so?"

Around ten o'clock that night we were allowed to accompany Mummy back to the Toppins to see how the cakes had turned out. They looked exactly as we were accustomed to seeing black cake look at our home. One last batch was in the oven. Mummy had saved the day.

## *Chapter Fourteen*

That Dell was really leaving for England was reinforced when on Thursday before I started Community College an employee of the internet provider climbed the pole outside our yard and made a connection to our house. When Dell came home, she informed me that she had bought a computer and signed me up for some classes. It was time I started familiarizing myself with the technology and stop living in the Dark Ages of letter writing now known as snail mail. She was sure Tessa was doing Computer at school and I would need it for 'A' Level. The machine was delivered and installed the next day, on the newly assembled computer desk in our room. Then the printer was also installed. This all looked so final, I cried.

"You silly goat," Dell said hugging me. "I am making sure we can chat every day! It'll be like I'm still here!"

With encouragement like that I determined to master the crash course, so by the completion of my first week of actual classes at College, I felt confident e-mailing, using Microsoft Word and using the search engines. Now Dell and I discussed her study plans without my becoming tearful. I sat beside her as she compared accommodations available online and made queries.

We thought we were cruising safely to end of year when the curse of the Leap Year surfaced again. Granny was in the backyard clearing her peas plants of weeds and Dell and I were toting the weeds to the pile for composting one Saturday afternoon when we heard sounds of quarrelling in the road at the front. Of course we didn't dare investigate. I was sweating with the effort to stay put when Miss Estellita Joe, dress torn halfway across her shoulder, ran into the yard, followed by Miss Bernice King with scratches on her face and arms.

"No! No! No! Not in here!" Granny shouted to no avail, gesturing with her cutlass in hand.

Everything else happened swiftly.

Miss Estellita ran to Granny and snatched the cutlass from her surprised grasp. Miss Bernice reached Miss Estellita, grabbed her hand, pried the cutlass from her clutch and swiftly delivered an expert "planning" to her legs and behind. Then she threw the cutlass through the half-opened window of Granny's garden shed, dusted off her hands and placing them akimbo, faced Miss Estellita again.

All Granny could say was, "But you see my trials and crosses this evening!"

Mummy arrived at the living room window in time to see some villagers restraining Miss Estellita and taking her out of the yard. Miss Bernice walked behind, still breathing hard.

Sure enough on Monday morning a Constable from the Calliaqua Police Station appeared to take a statement from Granny and according to her, deprive her of the lawful use of her cutlass. We knew that meant that someone had reported the matter to the police, and it was likely that Granny would be called as a witness. Constable Williams had taken the cutlass as evidence. No one had been injured in the fracas so Granny hoped the case would be heard quickly enough so she could get back her cutlass.

To my surprise, Miss Estellita and Miss Bernice were coming out of our yard when I returned from school on Wednesday afternoon. They were chucking each other and slapping each other on the shoulder and laughing! Mummy was on the porch shaking her head.

On reading witness statements and the complainant's reports, fatherly Station Sergeant Adams had called Miss Estellita and Miss Bernice to his office and reprimanded them. He had secured a promise from them that they would conduct themselves properly and go apologize to Mrs. Matthews. Miss Estellita had seen the wisdom of dropping the case and in a show of good faith, Station Sergeant Adams had entrusted them with the cutlass to return to Granny with their apologies.

Mummy said that was the funniest thing she had seen in a long time. They had brought the cutlass wrapped in the flour bag in which the Constable had taken it, and after tripping over themselves apologizing, they had left together as friends again.

And Granny was still shaking her head and saying, "But you see my trials and crosses this evening!"

## *Chapter Fifteen*

It was close to the end of first semester. I felt good about my subjects which had been selected primarily to avoid Maths and secondly because I really didn't know what I wanted as a career.

Psychology was interesting, but a lot of work. We had case studies for every concept. Access to the computer at home was a real asset. Literature was my pet subject and Spanish and Geography were manageable. Since Caribbean Studies was a one-year course, Tedica and I had begged the lecturer to sign us up and we didn't want to let her down. I found that the more time I spent reading on my subjects, the easier it was for me to follow the lecturers. I guess that is what studying does.

Best of all, now that we were online, I could send messages to Tessa every day and sometimes we met online to chat. She got the news the same day; no more two-week wait!

I was in the Library catching up on some Caribbean Studies reading one hot November afternoon when I suddenly started trembling violently. No, the earth was trem...!

"Earthquake!" By the time the realization settled on me I was through the door and in the yard. The jingle, 'Drop, cover and hold! Stay in control!' was just that in my mind - a jingle. Other students, staff and administrative personnel had scrambled from the buildings and were gathered in the yard waiting for the tremor to subside. The vehicles parked in the yard were rocking from side to side like *Admiral* going through the Bequia Channel in December. There was much screaming because the quake didn't seem to want to stop. Eventually it did, and the Dean sent word that classes were suspended for the rest of the day. It was almost three o'clock anyway. I quickly returned to the library for my bag and textbooks and headed home. People were sharing experiences in the Vale.

Mummy said she was at the machine just finishing a garment when she realized that she was rocking in her seat and things were falling around her. She had waited a while, but when the shaking hadn't stopped, she had run through the kitchen door and into the yard. Granny wasn't home; out somewhere on a mission of mercy, as usual. Dell said everybody in her office took to the street at the first rattling of furniture.

I was asking Mummy what's for lunch when we heard someone calling in the front yard.

"Miss Craigg! Miss Craigg!" Mummy went out to meet Miss Katherine. "If you see the Dunbars' house. I don't see how they could ever live in that!"

She explained that some blocks had fallen out of the top part of the structure and that the rest of the building looked unsafe.

That reminded me that Tessa had said that the Dunbars were still in occupation of the house that had belonged to Great Aunt Melanie and they were still unable to get their money from Lawyer Smith. I really had to go look at the house.

As Miss Katherine had said, the structure indeed looked unsafe. Other villagers were also looking at the misshapen structure. Although the materials delivered by the first government truck had remained there, work towards completion of the building had not recommenced. With elections not far away, they must have recognized that something needed to be done, but they were probably wary of the villagers.

That Saturday afternoon instead of taking the shortcut to Young Peoples, Dell and I walked the main road. As we passed the Dunbars' residence I observed that we had never seen the elder daughter and maybe we should invite her to YPs.

"She's not around," Dell responded.

"What d'you mean?" I inquired, not hiding my surprise.

"Got a scholarship and went off to study."

"How d'you know?" I persisted.

"Office talk," Dell muttered. She seemed unwilling to continue on that topic so I backed off.

This was the last weekend before elections so everybody was out on the campaign trail. Several vehicles with amplified sounds had already passed us on the road. There was so much noise in the vicinity of church that the Youth Director decided to abandon YPs until next Saturday. Dell and I retraced out steps, heading back home. As we passed the Dunbars again, they were just taking groceries from the car in the garage to the kitchen. Did I say Mrs. Dunbar looked around Mummy's age? Not true! She looked older than Granny and tired too. She was reaching into the vehicle and had just taken out two black plastic bags when Mr. Dunbar came back through the kitchen door, slammed it behind him, barked something at her, and jumping into the driver's seat revved the vehicle into reverse and into the yard. Then with the vehicle facing forward, he sped towards the main road and scratched off up the road.

"Wow!" Dell and I exclaimed simultaneously. I dusted gravel from my hair.

"He's in a foul mood," I stated the obvious. We hurried back home with hardly any further exchange.

Granny was on the phone when we got home.

"Uncle Marcus," Mummy mouthed.

When the call ended Granny said, "That was Uncle Marcus. He said that since you're going to be attending that business school in Guildford he will not hear of your moving into "digs" over there. He is ten minutes' drive away and on the bus route so he and Aunt Annesta would be more than happy to have you live with them." She waited for Dell to respond. "Well?"

"That's fine," Dell replied as expected. She didn't sound completely convinced though. That was confirmed when she queried, "Aren't they the older Uncle and Auntie?"

"As old as I am," Granny replied, "but they kept well. Andrew and Sonia live and work in London and come by regularly."

"Oh! I remember now. They are Andrew and Sonia's grandparents."

I remembered them too. Their one daughter and her husband had been killed by a drunk driver. The children were about six and eight at the time, so Uncle Marcus and Aunt Annesta had raised them.

"Okay, then I would just make a contribution to living expenses," Dell said. Granny nodded her approval. Everybody seemed satisfied with the arrangements. The deadline for making a deposit to the Housing Unit was the following Monday, so Dell went to send them an e-mail cancelling her housing request. I followed and forgot about the Dunbars that night.

*******************

Ever so often one encounters someone like Miss Maureen. She was one of those people who minded their business, but she was also gifted with a caring disposition that wooed one's confidence. She was mostly quietly respectful and friendly, but like those people so disposed, she did not "skylark."

She lived alone in her little house which was about eight houses up the road from ours. It was near to a location where commuters waited for transportation out of town under the shade of a huge hog plum tree. Miss Maureen's mother, Annette, had seized the opportunity to migrate to Canada under a Home Help Program, leaving her to be raised by her grandmother Miss Eulalie. Upon the passing of Miss Eulalie, Miss Maureen's uncle Terrence made it his business to drop by regularly as usual, doing little repairs around the house and generally making sure that everyone knew there was a male presence in the house and that Miss Maureen was comfortable.

Miss Maureen swept her yard with a bamboo broom, and along what I presumed to be her boundaries, she had rows of used tires which she kept painted white. In them she planted a variety of herbs. I could smell mint, and her thick leaf thyme rebelled against confinement to its container despite being cut back for making her seasoning. Off to the left side of the front of the yard, Miss Maureen had got Uncle Terry to build her a small wooden shop from which she sold her bottled seasoning and pepper sauce, coconut sugar cakes, ginger sticks and tamarind balls when tamarinds were in season. She had also added a good-sized cooler in which she kept her fruit popsicles – guava, sour sop, cherry, and five finger. I had no qualms about buying her popsicles. Her place was always clean and Granny said they were good people. She remembered Miss Eulalie as a senior at Belair Primary school.

The shop was painted a light blue on the outside and a light green inside. It stood on a square concrete foundation and was constructed so that the front opening and the counter receded when it was closed. Miss Maureen spent most of her time in her kitchen preparing her items for sale. She opened the shop mostly on afternoons, attracting the patronage of school children, and adults who favoured her seasonings.

Monday was the day before Election Day, and although it is not clear exactly who had provoked Miss Maureen, it is presumed that the culprit was a politician or someone connected, as the majority of the politicians and the most vocal supporters travelled to town from the windward side of the island. There is nothing extraordinary about a white t-shirt and black hot pants accessorized by black fishnet stockings on an attractive lady, but Miss Maureen caused a major traffic jam and no small excitement for the commuters on the road that Monday morning. An undisputed black beauty, she struck a pose in her little porch wearing her white t-shirt on which was painted a huge pair of very red pursed lips. I remembered seeing Miss Maureen in that t-shirt on several occasions during the last week and I had thought then that she either really liked the t-shirt or it was some sort of uniform. Now, when I saw Uncle Terry's donkey with a similar t-shirt pulled taut over its rump and munching contentedly on the dewy grass just outside Miss Maureen's property, things all fell into place. I would recognize that donkey anywhere. That was Rhoda and she was a regular feature at the annual fair and concert of the Sion Hill Government School. Children paid fifty cents for a donkey ride around the playing field.

The message was unmistakable. If the concept were transferred to cardboard, Miss Maureen would easily have won in her category at J'ouvert. The other subliminal message was, "Do not interfere with people like Miss Maureen."

On my way to school to pay a library fine, I lingered under the hog plum tree to see what the two constables who arrived on the scene would do, but they just waved the traffic along as best they could. I smiled as I counted five more identical t-shirts on Miss Maureen's clothes line soaking up the morning sunlight in the brisk breeze in her backyard.

On Tuesday morning, Miss Maureen was just ahead of Dell as she made her way to the polling station to vote for the first time. Dell was dressed for work, but Miss Maureen was now demurely attired in a white cotton shirt, tan trousers and black sandals. In combination with her purposeful stride, she was smiling the smile of one who had successfully accomplished every aspect of a major feat. Yesterday's caper had obviously reached its target!

Like most of the village, Dell and I stayed up looking at the TV coverage of the election results. The Conservative Democratic Party won a landslide victory, so Wednesday was declared a national holiday. The Party travelled the entire country thanking the electorate for reposing such confidence in them and promising to set the country on a steady course to economic recovery and stability. The Revolutionary Labour Party were sore losers and promised to do all in their power to thwart the efforts of the new government. The candidates for the Party for Social Preservation and the Progressive Movement for Social Unity all lost their deposits.

## *Chapter Sixteen*

Life settled back to normal. Somewhere in my subconscious I was rejoicing that the leap year was coming to a close without further distress, having long since declassified Dell's departure for England as calamity. She was leaving early Sunday morning so we were having the YPs and some of her office friends over initially for cheesecake and ice-cream the Friday evening after work.

Mummy and I were putting the porch "ship shape" according to her, when we noticed some unusual activity taking place at our neighbours' obliquely opposite us. Claire Audain drove into her yard and then closed shut their newly installed wrought iron gate. She fastened the gate further with a length of chain and secured all that with a lock the size of one of Granny's expensive China saucers. Then she sat on the porch calmly crocheting. Mummy pretended not to be looking, but at one time I saw her trying to smother a smile. Now I was more curious than ever.

The Audains were original villagers. Claire was formerly a Solomon and lived with her parents until they passed on. She had two children for Wilmot but continued living at home until his mother passed. They had then married and she rented out her place and moved into his. Their third child was born shortly after. Courtney was about eighteen now, a wiry athletic type who played football and cricket. He was always out representing the country somewhere. The elder two who were about eighteen months apart were in Atlanta with an Auntie Jen while they studied engineering.

Recently the Audains had enclosed their property, more for aesthetic value than for barricade and security, and had spent long evenings together planting flowering shrubs and installing garden lights that were solar operated. But as old people say, "House roof does cover down plenty."

Not long after Claire had secured the gate, Wilmot drew up in his blue Pajero and surveyed the scene. Claire did not move. Wilmot came out of the Pajero and stood at the gate. Still no action from Claire. He returned to the Pajero and wound up the glass. I presumed he had the AC running.

Dell came home from work and we kept an eye on the Audains between fixing a table with finger foods near the front door. When the guests started arriving, Wilmot was still in the Pajero. Darkness fell and he was still in the jeep. The guests were unaware of the drama playing out outside, but we were stealthily keeping track as we imagined were the other neighbours on the street. By nine o'clock our guests were saying their goodbyes and climbing into their vehicles. The lights in the garden at the Audains were aglow and Wilmot was still outside in his Pajero. Dell, Mummy and I cleaned up and turned off our porch lights leaving Wilmot in the glow of his garden lights.

"I wonder why he's not going over the fence," I said to no one in particular. "I could hurdle that easily," I said.

"He probably has good reason," Granny remarked. "And good night," she added.

We went to bed and left poor Wilmot parked outside his gate. I figured if he didn't turn off the vehicle he would run out of gas before morning. Good thing Saturday wasn't a working day for him.

*****************************

The gate was still locked and the Pajero was still outside when we started our Saturday morning. People on our street went about their business as usual. Well, everybody on the street pretended. We were all keeping an eye on the unfolding Audain saga.

Claire came out of the front door, unlocked the gate and put the chain and lock in the trunk of her car then crossed the road to our neighbours.

"Good morning, Glenda, Marlon. How you doing?" We heard her shout. Glenda and Marlon came out on their porch and they chatted for about half hour then she came to our yard.

"Miss Matthews, good morning!"

Granny went out to the porch with Dell and me right behind her.

"Hi Claire!" Granny turned and fixed us with her petrifying stare, but Claire objected.

"It's all right. I want everybody to know. I am telling everybody," she stated calmly. She repeated, articulating each syllable, "Every body."

"Yesterday I saw Wilmot go to the house of a woman in Calliaqua instead of coming straight home after work."

"Okay," Granny prompted.

"I had heard the rumour and when I asked him, he denied it. But yesterday I saw him go up to the house and knock. She barely opened the door and held him by his tie and pulled him inside. When he didn't come out after a good half hour, I went shopping and locked the gate." She took a deep breath. "Miss Matthews, I done with being a wife! He could do what he want! I am going next door to tell them. I will tell everybody I know." So saying, Claire went over to the neighbours' yard.

"Oh Lord, Claire is so calm, please don't let her have a nervous breakdown," Granny prayed.

After that we really went about our Saturday morning business. Dell was leaving early next morning.

We all trouped to the airport to send Dell off. She checked in, cleared Immigration, and then came back out. At the last call from LIAT she scrambled back in to clear Customs and rush through the Departure Lounge. We were too many to flock to the airport fence.

Back home we got ready for church which was scheduled for nine o'clock. Evening service was scheduled for ten o'clock as it was Old Year's Day. I knew where I was expected to be at midnight.

Granny prayed again for the entire country. Dell, Uncle Marcus and Aunt Annesta were included and Claire and Wilmot got special mention.

********************

Going into second semester meant that the heat was on, so Dell had helped me set up a study timetable and I was sticking to it. I was working with an island scholarship in mind.

January moved swiftly into February. Dell had settled in and was even doing some sightseeing on her own when Andrew and Sonia were not around, she said. She, Steven and Tessa were online almost daily. Sometimes we sent e-mails, but at other times we connected via Skype. One day I regaled them with the story of the lady who called a talk show host to lament the loss of her handbag to the garbage collectors. Her prefacing her complaint with, "Yuh think is right that the garbage people should go way wid me handbag?" gave rise to a flood of derisive comments. Prompted by the host, the caller had gone on to explain that it was garbage collection day in her area. The authorities say that householders should put out their garbage by six o'clock on the morning of collection, but they never come at that time. When she came out shortly after eight o'clock, ready to go to town, the garbage truck was just coming up the road with their usual noise and flinging people's bins about. She just put down her handbag as she bent down to buckle her sandals, and when she looked up again the garbage bag she had put out since half past five that morning was gone and so were her handbag and the garbage truck! Before I could tell Dell and Tessa what listeners had called to suggest, they were laughingly making the very same comments! The host himself had tried without success to lend a controlled, sympathetic ear, but he gave up completely when the caller conceded that it was a good thing she had had her ID and bus fare tied up in a 'kerchief in her bosom!

Then Miss Rosita's neighbours, the Thorpes, were conned out of fifty dollars one day. They were in charge of a plot of land that separated their properties. The Thomases, who were the owners, were overseas and had left them in charge. Miss Rosita had suggested to the Thorpes that they work the land together, sell the produce, share the profits and put aside something for the owners to pay the taxes.

"No," Miss Thorpe had stoutly rejected the suggestion. "They put us in charge; they never said work it!" Miss Rosita could not convince her that it made sense to cultivate the plot, so she gave up. Along came a young man one day when the grass had grown uncomfortably high. He asked for the job to trim the bush.

"How much you would do it for?" Miss Thorpe enquired.

They settled for seventy-five dollars and he was to trim it dirt-low and pile up the trash in the corner where it could be composted later.

At mid-morning the young man called out to Miss Thorpe. Could she advance him fifty dollars as he wanted to buy some items for the mistress to cook for when the children came home for lunch? Miss Thorpe went inside and returned with the fifty dollars for the young man. That was the last she saw of him.

Miss Rosita told her, on hearing the story, that the young man lived in a two by four in Belmont and he had neither mistress nor children.

Dell's firm wasn't faring too well in the Firms' and Industrial Netball Competition. They were close to the bottom of the enthusiastic competitors. My shouting myself hoarse at their games did little to help, so I gave up and concentrated on my books. First year exams were fast approaching.

I was on the bridge taking the long route to YPs one Saturday afternoon when Lawyer Smith crossed my mind. Then as though I had conjured him up, a long silver-grey car drove past with him sitting in the passenger seat and wearing a medical collar. His son was driving. When I passed the Dunbars' the same silver-grey car was parked in the yard. I got an instant headache.

The last time I had heard about Tessa's Great Aunt Melanie's plight, Lawyer Smith had still not paid them any money. I had said to myself then, "Some people never learn!" And then I had chuckled aloud. I was beginning to sound like Granny.

When I arrived at YPs I was preoccupied with thoughts of Granny. She wasn't as young as she used to be. I was still a baby when Grandpa passed away. Granny and Mummy were all I knew as parents. I got all choked up thinking about life without her. I went through the motions of being at YPs but nothing much registered that evening. I was still in a brown study when I approached home having hustled through the shortcut. It looked like all the lights in the house were on.

## *Chapter Seventeen*

Mummy and Granny were waiting in the porch. They looked me over somberly and then told me to sit. I sat.

"Your father passed away this afternoon," Mummy announced. "We were waiting for you to come home so you could tell Dell."

I didn't respond. What could I say? My father was a nebulous character who seemed not to care about our existence and we managed well without him, I thought. When I was a toddler my parents had divorced and Mummy had moved back home with Granny. In the settlement, since he was at fault, the Court had ordered him to pay maintenance for Mummy, Dell and me. He went to Court so often asking that the amount be reduced that Mummy got tired and decided that she could do without the annoyance. He left the country and we had not heard about him again for a long time. At some time while I was growing up, I had wondered about him and had looked at every father-figure trying to identify some feature of resemblance to me. I had heard somewhere that children bore some resemblance to their parents and that I resembled my father. That diversion was short-lived. There were so many other interesting pursuits in which to involve oneself. Remarried and with a ready-made family, my father had returned home some months ago in poor health and had passed away earlier this afternoon at his home.

Now it seemed as though I was expected to make some response, so I said, "Oh! Okay!"

We went inside and I booted up the computer to try for Dell. She wasn't online so I sent an e-mail that we would be on again at nine.

I still had not stopped to analyze my feelings at my father's passing. I honestly didn't know how to react to the passing of someone who played a minor role in my existence. He obviously had the means to provide for his family but chose not to do so. Mummy worked night and day as a seamstress to ensure our financial survival, but we were primarily dependent on Granny's kitchen garden and Grandpa's little survivor's pension from his job with the oil company in Curaçao.

When we finally got hold of Dell and she was informed, her immediate response was, "What do you want me to do?"

I could see that Mummy and Granny were stumped for a while and then Mummy said, "Whatever you want to. We just thought you should know."

"Oh! Okay!" Dell said.

And then we talked about other things and let the girl go back to her studies.

When I lay in my bed that night, I thought how terrible it must be that we didn't feel any sadness at the demise of our biological father. A week later, Mummy went to the funeral. Granny stayed at home with me.

## *Chapter Eighteen*

With first year exams just weeks away, I concentrated on my studies to the exclusion of all else. I was determined to ace my Communication Studies oral presentation, so I had been working diligently on it since January. I was examining the topic, "The Effects of Single Parenting on the Young People in my School Community." It was an ambitious project, but there were so many of us, I decided to try, especially since I was also doing Psychology. Of the six of us, only DeDe lived with both parents. Their topics had Management and Economics biases because they were focused more on Business Studies. Tedica was also from a single parent home. She had mixed Business and Spanish as she was aiming at a scholarship to a Spanish speaking country. We got together and practised our presentations using our check lists to ensure that we had covered all the elements. We meant business!

My surname being Craigg, I was amongst the first students to present. The experience was numbing. When I made the comment, DeDe affirmed, "Tell me about it! Miss and Sir just sat there and looked at me without one expression on their faces! Good thing we had practised in the mirror too! I decided to pretend I was looking in the mirror and seeing two people."

Rodney stated emphatically, "Based on the criteria, we should all get full marks for our orals."

After the orals we stayed glued to our books until mid-June when written exams were completed.

Then we decided to strategize. College was deadly, so we decided to approach second year way ahead of the pack. While others were talking about vacation overseas and the different diversions for the long holidays, we were busy downloading our various syllabuses and spending time in the Public Library. We noted the areas of concern to ask our lecturers about and worked steadily on the topics that we could handle on our own. It was hard work and I felt so ravenous by mid-morning that we made it a practice of having break at regular school break-time and then back to the books until three o'clock. On our way back to the Library after buying snacks one morning we encountered a former teacher who singled me out for criticism.

"Vaughna Craigg! Where are you spreading going so?" Miss Wills inquired. Don't ask if I was mortified. Considering that Miss Wills herself was as fat as a toothpick, Mummy and Granny would have been immeasurably proud of me that I held my tongue. The others too went quiet and then somebody said cheerfully, "Nah Miss, she looks hot!"

I couldn't wait to get home. I tried on last term's school clothes and they were fitting just fine, but I thought I would "make assurance doubly sure," a tried and tested expression of Granny's. I set about making a lap around the neighbourhood on mornings and skipping in the backyard on evenings.

After doing a lap around the house, I would run on the road, up the 'gouti track' at the other end of the village, along another strip of road and then down another 'gouti track' at the other end of the village and onto the road that would take me back home. The entire run usually took half an hour and I finished off with a lap around the house before skipping up the steps and flopping into the chair in the porch.

On this morning, I raced into the yard, cleared the living room side of the house and the bedrooms and was heading to the kitchen side when I encountered a sight that is carved indelibly in my memory. Wilmot Audain was sitting on the back door step near the outside sink bawling, snot running from his nose as he tried to wipe his eyes with the tail of his shirt.

"Ah … can't take it no more, Miss Matt," he was sobbing. Granny was sitting beside him, looking at him. She looked up and fixed me with "the glare" that had me back pedaling out of sight again. That was the end of my exercising for the morning. When I had finally caught my breath, I went looking for Mummy to tell her what I had seen. It reminded me about the last part of Matthew 26: 75 that said that Peter 'wept bitterly.'

Mummy said, "Well, yes. It seems he is really sorry, but Claire is not relenting."

"Wow! I didn't know men could cry so!" I was still in a state of wonder.

Breakfast was difficult. Granny had still not come in, so I was wary about stirring in the kitchen lest she thought I was peeping. Finally, I had some cereal and some tea and then took myself off to the Library for the day. I knew Mummy would fill me in on anything that transpired in my absence.

## *Chapter Nineteen*

In the last week of August, results were released and just as Rodney had predicted, we all did well in our exams. As the weather was holding fine, we spent some time on the beach between doing final preparations for school, and September morning found us ready for second year.

September and October produced one tropical weather system after the other with intervals of blistering heat and cool breezy days. By mid-November when Christmas breezes started in earnest, villagers had their windows and doors wide open to let them in.

After having spent the night before rolling about on my bed in agony, I didn't exactly feel civil next morning. I had a two-thirty class, so I crawled around the house lethargically and then wandered onto the porch.

"Kookooyookoo!" The rooster trumpeted for about the fiftieth time in the last half hour. Granny had had enough.

"Look here!" she shouted from the porch, "If you don't keep less noise in my head, I will wring your neck and cook you!" she warned.

"Kookooyookoo!" the roster responded and strutted to the other side of the road out of Granny's reach but facing the house.

"Kookooyookoo!" he taunted, flapping his way along the Audains' fence.

"Ten o'clock in the morning and that cock behaving like that. It is either somebody we haven't seen for a long time coming here or some young girl is pregnant!"

"Well, don't look in my direction," I protested with ill humour. "That is not supposed to happen again according to the Bible."

Granny sucked her teeth in annoyance, a practice against which she had repeatedly warned us, and retreated to the kitchen. Now amused, I sat on the porch wall and watched the rooster continue to defy my grandmother.

I had been sitting there for another good twenty minutes and was now in agreement with Granny that the rooster was overdoing a good joke when a well-dressed middle-aged gentleman appeared. Unexplainably, I immediately felt the tug of kinship ties.

"Good day!" he hailed, confidently climbing the steps. Granny came out of the front door simultaneously. The stranger smiled broadly and folded her in a hug. "Aunt Ethel!" he beamed. Mummy joined us in the porch. Granny looked hard at him. "You can't be...."

"Uncle Neville's grandson, Morrison," he supplied. I caught myself staring, unable to shake the uncanny feeling that I knew this person although we had obviously never met.

"And you must be Cousin Elaine," he said engulfing Mummy with a huge hug. Granny invited him in, and I trailed behind them. Before accepting the offered seat, he looked from me to Mummy and declared, "Your mother's own child!"

In my most ladylike manner I said, "Yes, I am Vaughna," as I extended my hand for a shake. His grasp was firm and warm and then I was drawn into a hug too. We settled down in the living room and I spent an enthralling hour or so listening as my parents recounted the exploits of family members, some of whom I had never heard.

Cousin Morrison stayed for lunch and then we moved out on to the porch. We learned that after graduating from UWI St. Augustine, he had gone to England for further studies and there had married a young nurse from St. Kitts. His job as an engineer had taken him to Africa for a year in the first instance when Morrison Jr. was still a toddler. During the next seven years they had had two more children, Jessica and Phillippe, he had done another Africa stint and he had also earned his doctorate. Morrison Jr. had followed in his steps and was already a civil engineer while Jessica had taken to nursing like her mother.

Phillippe, like me, was about to finish his 'A' Levels and like me was undecided about his career path.

"So what brings you here now?" Granny inquired. He was all smiles again. I liked him.

"Well, I've been on assignment in the BVI for the past three years, backwards and forwards, you know, and I got to hankering for a piece of the rock, so I bought a property on the other side of the village." He grinned again.

I was now on the edge of my seat. "You bought the Marshalls' property," I stated. Mummy and Granny had obviously come to the same conclusion before he nodded.

"So what's to happen now?" Granny asked.

Cousin Morrison laughed. "I wrote a letter to the electricity company requesting disconnection of the service as the new owner–included documentary proof and all. They did disconnect, but it seems the squatter has his own connections, so the service was restored." He raised his eyebrows quizzically. "Then from the water people I got the most interesting response that they couldn't disconnect the service because if there are young children there and they became ill from lack of sanitation, they, the water people, would be liable!" He was laughing and shaking his head.

"Hmmm!" Mummy and Granny muttered.

"Aunt Ethel, it's going to take a lot more than politicians and cronyism to deter me from enjoying this land of my birth! As soon as the children are settled, Flora and I are moving back to this rock!"

I was still in awe from all the information I had acquired and was anxious to share with Dell and Tessa.

"So where are you off to now?" Mummy seemed to have found her voice.

"Back to Cousin Horace's for the time being." There was some more family talk and then Cousin Morrison took his leave after another round of hugging and promising to pop by again before returning to England. As usual with Granny, she fixed up a package of cocoa and guava cheese for him to carry with him. Visitors never left our house empty handed.

Not a thought of school had passed my mind all day!

## *Chapter Twenty*

As promised, Cousin Morrison returned before leaving for England. He was going home for Christmas. An envelope with some pounds sterling changed hands at some time during the visit.

"For Christmas," he said, and Granny packed up more delicacies for him and went to the airport the next day to see him off. He had suggested that Phillippe come to the "land of his ancestry" after his 'A'Levels exams and I was looking forward to that.

Throughout the Christmas season, only two groups of serenaders showed up singing carols. One was a mature group of men from the village with their banjo, guitar, quatro, mouth organ, drum and shak-shak. And one man actually whistled two whole verses of 'Silent Night.' They made plenty noise, but they sang well and delivered a speech to which each member of the band contributed. I enjoyed that. If Granny and Mummy's donation is any measure of their satisfaction with the group's performance, they were as pleased as I was. The other group identified themselves as the Young People from a church in Belair. They mostly had recorders as their musical instruments and one enterprising young lady had a comb. She must have run out of wax paper because before they left, she pulled me aside and asked in a whisper if I had any to spare. I ran to the kitchen and quickly rolled off a piece of Cut-Rite for her. At the same time, I remembered that I had found three dollars in my pants pocket the week before, so I scooped them off the top of the fridge and handed them to her. The group looked tired, but they had done well. To me, serenading was an important part of Christmas.

Christmas finally arrived and we called Dell on Skype, spending a long time chatting and pointing out what changes had taken place. She had vowed to have only one meal of "spuds" per week in the upcoming year as that heavily potato diet seemed to be lodging itself firmly to her hips and buttocks. "I am going to have to go to a gym to try and shake it loose," she grinned showing us the evidence.

"That's fine," I responded. "When you decide to go shopping, you could just buy another outfit like the one you're wearing. I know somebody who it will fit nicely!"

My share of Cousin Morrison's envelope had turned out to be a whole twenty-pound note. I started making all kinds of plans for it; I put it away and forgot where.

Our Old Year's routine hadn't changed, and Dell didn't escape.

Granny had told me to let her know that she would expect her to make herself available for prayer at midnight our time. Poor Dell was a sight to behold! Uncle Marcus and Aunt Annesta joined her and then everybody had to be brought up to date about Cousin Morrison who had passed by to deliver some of Granny's goodies to them.

It seemed that once the New Year started it was in a great hurry to get to an end. January raced into February.

*********************

Before the morning news was aired, news reached us that the Dunbars' building was falling apart. A good-sized piece had fallen into the yard the night before. The news reported that the seismograph in Trinidad had registered a slight tremor that had extended throughout the Eastern Caribbean. No damage had been reported, the newscaster stated. The villagers knew better, but nobody said anything. As a matter of fact, people knew that the structure was a hazard and wondered why the authorities didn't condemn it. If the Dunbars went there, they did so under cover of total darkness, for nobody ever saw them.

I had begun to lose interest in them, but the knowledge that the house they were occupying belonged to family stimulated it once more. And then Tedica shared some information with me. Although she worshipped on a Saturday, she would often come to church with me on special occasions and sometimes showed up at YPs. When we passed the Dunbars' on our way to Easter Sunday special there didn't seem to be any activity at the house.

"You know we had Convention at the Park yesterday?" Tedica started up.

"Yes. How did that go?" I inquired.

"The usual," she replied. "Got to see a lot of friends from the other districts. But that came afterwards."

"Huh?" I prompted.

"When we passed here yesterday, there was quite a crowd here."

"What on earth are you talking about?" I demanded.

"So you didn't hear? Ronald Dunbar put a licking on his father yesterday morning."

"For real? How come?" Tedica could be so annoying at times! I wanted to know and we were nearly at church.

"Well, based on what I saw, I would say that Dunbar must have been abusing the wife and Ronald took matters into his own hands."

"What exactly did he do and how come you know his name?"

"He had him up against the garage wall punching him in the face and telling him not to hit his mother again. That was one angry boy!"

"For real?"

"Yep! And when Dunbar eventually got away, he ran to the vehicle, but Ron grabbed him again. More licks!"

"And nobody stopped him?"

"Couldn't. He had to get it all out," Tedica responded. "Then Ron took the piece of pipe from under the driver's side mat of the jeep and stood in the yard waiting. Mr. Dunbar scrambled into the vehicle and sped away."

"And all this time nobody intervened?"

"Wasn't time. Whole show couldn't have lasted more than three minutes."

"You took more than five minutes to tell me," I complained. "And you still haven't told me how you know his name."

"Somebody in the crowd was calling out to him."

"So they must have gone to cool off," I suggested. "Over there's very quiet. Where were the mother and young child all this time?"

"In the house, I imagine," Tedica responded.

We arrived at church. The YPs programme about the Resurrection Story was well received. The adults played their part with a real Brother John outrunning a real Brother Peter to get to the sepulchre in the short Resurrection skit. After the entire service, each child received a tiny basket with ginger cookies and chocolates.

When we passed the Dunbars again, the windows were opened but there was no vehicle in the yard.

"So if she is being abused, I wonder why she is staying," I wondered aloud as we passed.

"Especially in this day and age when domestic violence is discussed openly," Tedica added. "He probably has some hold on her."

"Sad," I murmured. I thought he must be some kind of beast. Tedica and I parted ways at her junction and I continued on my way home.

## *Chapter Twenty-One*

Although I had done well in year one at College, now that finals were approaching, I felt anxious. There was much at stake. The competition for the few scholarships was keen, not only within my own circle of friends, but also amongst other students. Of course, there were those who would be satisfied with just passing and then there were still others who didn't care either way, and treated College as their primary socialization venue.

As soon as Easter holidays were over, we resumed our group studies. Dell organized for me a study timetable based on my exam schedule, and the group used that to craft their individual study timetables. I reserved time for church and YPs and some "Vaughna time" and still managed to get at least seven hours' sleep every night.

Second year students were home for study period except for the occasional class that needed to meet to reinforce some concept. My classes had ceased, so I was reading some Psychology case studies when I became aware of feet running and loud garbled voices. Granny was already in the front yard and Mummy and I arrived in the porch almost together. Mummy's questioning expression and gesture yielded the response, "A man take off down the airstrip!"

My jogging route took me along a vantage point that afforded me a clear view of the airstrip. The crowd was running in the direction of the airport. I barely heard Mummy's, "Where…." as I darted out of the yard and headed for the 'gouti track' down which I would normally travel on the final leg of my run home. I took the hill zigzagging up the incline and was soon at the top. Villagers living along the way were either at work or had not heard what was happening below, but my appearance attracted attention.

"What…?" one started to ask.

"A man on the airstrip," I panted.

Arms and legs pumping with mechanical precision and speed, a male figure was moving down the runway like greased lightning. The airport fire truck and an Airport Security vehicle were in pursuit, but nowhere near. Shining metallic sparks flashed from the vehicles as they accelerated down the strip, but there was no catching him. Spectators were running on to the strip for a better view and police officers stationed at the airport were in vain trying to control them.

Suddenly the runner seemed to trip. Arms flailing like a windmill, he toppled head over heels and lay sprawled, face up on the tarmac. The Airport Security vehicle arrived on the spot then the Fire Truck trundled up. A number of villagers had joined me, and someone declared, "His heart mustbe burst with that speed!"

Another declared, "I going down!" and hurried off to access a shortcut down to the airport. The midmorning sun was intense so I eased myself into a space in the shade of a huge mango tree and sat down.

About ten minutes later an Ambulance screamed its way to the scene and medical personnel jumped out. Shortly after, they covered the body, returned to the vehicle and left the scene.

"He dead!" somebody announced. "Ambulance don't carry dead people."

Within another ten to fifteen minutes an open backed police vehicle drew up accompanied by a SUV which I presumed was a doctor's. He uncovered the body, spent some time in observation, then covered the body again and he too left the scene. The police seemed to be marking the spot. A hatch backed vehicle arrived. Then the covered body was placed on a gurney and shoved into the vehicle which sped away leaving the straggling spectators no alternative but to return to wherever they had come from. The show was over, so the crowd reluctantly dispersed. As the sun was too hot for jogging, I hugged the shaded edges of the 'gouti track' and strolled home. Mummy was awaiting my return.

"What got into you to take off like that?" she wanted to know as soon as I reached the porch steps.

"I figured I could get a better view from the hill above the airport, and I did," I responded. I told her all that I had seen.

She was pensive. "I wonder who he is. He must have lost his mind to be running like that."

Granny was by her vegetable garden picking lettuce for our lunch plates. A young man was in the breadfruit tree having convinced Granny that he could reach the lone breadfruit on an extended branch halfway up the tree. Inching his way as far out on the branch as he dared, he hooked the breadfruit with the knife attached to a bamboo stick and when it fell, he grinned with satisfaction.

"Thanks. Come down now," Granny instructed. He dropped the stick and worked his way cautiously down to the ground. Granny fished a dollar from her pocket and offered it to the young man.

"Is all right, Miss Matt," he said. Granny was obviously surprised. "I good," he assured her.

"Who is your mother?" Granny asked.

"Miss Estellita," he responded, and taking up his tool bag, waved as he left the yard. "I good!"

"Well! Well! Well!" was all Granny could find to say.

The village was abuzz with the airport story, and by nightfall the identity of the runner was no longer a matter of speculation. The Evening's News confirmed his identity and the bits and pieces of the information we had been hearing all afternoon fell into place.

Just about seven years after the deed was done, lawyer number three in Nennie's property heist had inexplicably returned home. No one will ever know for sure what precipitated the action, but no sooner had his feet touched *terra firma* than the gentleman released his grasp on his carry-on bag, raced past the baggage handlers at the back of the aircraft, on to the runway, and took off before anyone realized what was happening. I had seen the rest.

Of course Dell and Tessa had to be told of this latest development.

"How does one explain that?" Dell wanted to know. Granny's response was grim and decisive.

"Retribution!" she declared.

Glenda claimed that crossing the sea had delayed the retribution; returning had immediately restored it.

## *Chapter Twenty-Two*

My final exams started in mid-May and spread around in a most ungainly fashion. I knew I had aced Psychology, but the first Geography paper had me scrambling for my notes when I got home. I was focusing my preparation on Spanish and the next Geography paper, so had I failed either one, I would have had another reason not to like Mr. Dunbar.

The Jackson family lived in the vicinity of the Dunbars' maligned building. John Jackson was a carpenter by trade but dabbled in back yard gardening to supplement his earnings when work was slack. He had been in his garden that evening, but Miss May, a neighbour, had called him urgently to help her because her fowl coop was threatening to fall over. The repairs took longer than he had anticipated and it wasn't until he was ready for bed that he remembered that he had left his fork and cutlass in the back yard. He went for them. On his way to his back door he noticed activity at the Dunbars' place. It sounded like someone was pulling lumber across the floor. He mentioned his observations to his wife Peggy, but since the whole place was in darkness, they dismissed the matter. The next night they looked out because they heard a vehicle approaching in the dark.

When the vehicle stopped, the driver took something from the trunk and struggled up the steps. John called the police and reported suspicious activity at the Dunbars' place. The police took their time. When they did arrive, they found Mr. Dunbar on the floor unconscious. The contraptions around him indicated that he had built a scaffold and a makeshift ladder; was trying to attach a noose to the scaffold when he fell off the ladder bringing down the rest of the structure around him and knocking himself unconscious. He regained consciousness before the Ambulance arrived but looked disoriented. They strapped him, protesting, onto the stretcher and took off with him. The police took the scaffold, the makeshift ladder and the rope with them. All this information was courtesy Glenda who had come over to try on the dress Mummy was making for her, and I could hardly wait for nightfall to Skype Dell and Tessa with this latest piece of news.

I got Dell first, and after having dispensed with the usual preliminaries – how the family; how the weather; how the studies going – I broached the subject of the incident.

"Yes. I know." Dell muttered.

"You .... What? How did you hear that already? It happened night before last and we just heard today."

"Well .... Elena told me." Dell admitted sheepishly.

"How you mean ...? Who Elena?" I asked.

"Elena Dunbar."

"No, Dell. You are not playing fair!" I protested.

"Well …. It is all a bit delicate," she said hesitantly.

"But you never said you know the girl!" My disappointment was palpable.

"Yes, well …. I caught sight of her coming off a train that I was boarding some time ago."

"And you never said a word!" I accused. "Well?"

"Well what?" Dell's pretense at being obtuse was wearing my patience thin.

"Well what's the rest of the story? How did she come to be telling you things?" I almost screamed.

"She goes to the Guildford School of Nursing," Dell responded as though that answered any of my questions. I began to think she was doing this on purpose, just to annoy me and I decided not to let her.

"Hmm. So, you changed your course of studies and you chanced to meet in the College Canteen," I supplied mildly.

"No, you clown!" Dell had the nerve to chuckle. "Seriously, I actually met her in a restaurant at Piccadilly Circus in London. She looked so forlorn in that crowd, so I approached her as one Vincy to another and that is how I found out where she is studying. It's not far from my school."

"Okay." I prompted.

"Then we talked school and then home," Dell elaborated reluctantly. "We met a couple of times in Guildford after that and so it was one time she told me that her father had gone after her mother and her brother had made him sorry. That was after you had told me."

"I see," I observed. "And now?"

According to Dell, Elena had been trying to get her mother to leave her father since she had discovered that he had built a house for one concubine at home and was supporting another in Wisconsin. That is why he had arranged a scholarship for her; to get her out of the way, and now he is threatening to have it withdrawn.

"He could do that?" I asked.

"Maybe not now the government is changed," Dell suggested. "I don't really know how these things work, but the funding agency can't justify withdrawing funding if the student is doing well."

"And is she doing well?" I wanted to know.

"She is."

"So what is to happen now?"

"The mother is filing for a divorce."

"That's sad." I remembered having made that same comment

about that family before. As far as I was concerned, that was a truly sad family.

"Right. So that's why I was reluctant to say anything about it."

"Well, I hope meeting you helped to cheer her up," I encouraged. "Poor thing."

Granny and Mummy had their chats with Dell and I shut down the session. That whole exchange had eaten a significant chunk out of my study time, so I had to limit my chat time with Tessa to ten minutes. She understood. I was on my way to the bathroom before settling down to studies and was unaware that I had given voice to the thought that I was so disgusted with Mr. Dunbar to be seriously contemplating advising him to jump off his building next time. I felt Granny fix me with 'the glare' and turned when I heard the alarm in Mummy's voice as she called me by my whole name.

The opportunity never materialized. Planning authorities deemed the structure unsafe and had it razed.

## *Chapter Twenty-Three*

When exams were finished for me in the middle of the second week of June, I felt quite stunted. I stayed home sleeping for most of the days and the nights as well. The others seemed to have been similarly affected because I didn't hear much of them until well towards the end of the month. Tessa had been working extra hours for summer as part of her plan to save for travel the next year, so I had to settle for e-mails with her. I felt quite put out until Tedica offered to go to YPs with me that Saturday evening. We were making plans for Youth Camp, the venue for which was Grenada this year. The skit for talent night was being fine-tuned and the excitement was at a height. Additionally, since the sister churches were meeting for the annual inter-church fun and games competition on Carnival Tuesday, we had some strategizing to do. We were working for a hat-trick.

YPs started at 5:30 p.m. and officially ended at 7:30 p.m., but when Tedica and I eventually left church it was closer to eight o'clock. We were walking briskly past the Dunbars' house when we realized that they seemed to be moving. Furniture and boxes were being loaded onto a truck backed up to the kitchen door.

"Looks like they're moving, "I observed.

"Oh!" Tedica smothered the exclamation. I asked if she was all right and quickened my pace. It had begun to drizzle and the wind was blowing the raindrops right at us. I would be drenched by the time I got home if it persisted. When we parted at Tedica's junction I broke into a jog. All the lights were on at home, so I knew we had visitors. By the time I bounded up the porch steps and heard the unmistakable laughter, I knew who. Cousin Morrison was back! He and a younger version of himself rose to their feet as I entered.

"Hi, Cousin Morrison!" I greeted him and found myself in his arms. As soon as I was released, I was caught in another hug.

"Hi, Vaughna!"

"Hi, Phillippe!"

Phillippe was about seven inches taller than my five feet two inches and about my complexion. He wore his hair low or had had a haircut before travelling. He sounded so much like his father, I couldn't help liking him, immediately. Cousin Morrison was chuckling again.

"I kept my promise, but I guess I didn't have much choice. What does one do with a teenager who has finished school and doesn't know what to do?"

Phillippe laughed. "Take him on a Caribbean holiday!"

"Don't bank on it." Cousin Morrison countered. "You have work to do."

"Is nobody going to intervene on my behalf?" he appealed to the three of us.

"Well, all work and no play make Jack a dull boy, so I am sure you will be allowed some leisure," Granny smiled.

"You could hang out with us," I invited.

"They have work to do first," Mummy warned.

I informed them that I had seen the Dunbars moving out.

"Yes, so by mid-July the renovations should begin. I may yet be able to make a carpenter or mason out of him." Cousin Morrison raised his chin in the direction of his son and winked.

Mummy reminded me that I was wet, so making my excuses, I headed for a shower and change of clothes. I was already thinking of how I could rope Phillippe into my circle of friends. He sounded like fun.

When I returned, we sat in the porch and really got acquainted. We had quite a few interests that were similar. He had done a half marathon last summer; he liked reading and liked Shakespeare and he planned to soak up as much of the sea as he could. The long holidays were going to be fun!

## Chapter Twenty-Four

What makes seemingly rational parents do some totally irrational things sometimes? The question nagged at me long after the event. Years later, it resurfaced, and I was able to address it with the benefit of adulthood and find a clear and plausible answer.

I had had a drink of water and was just leaving the kitchen and heading towards my room when Granny called, "Vaughna, prepare yourself to go to the hospital with me tomorrow DV."

There is nothing wrong with my hearing, so I knew I had heard right. My immediate reaction was to ask why, but I also knew that would be futile, so I chose silence instead.

"Did you hear me?" Granny asked. We were now standing outside my bedroom door.

"Yes, Granny, but ...." I started.

"Just do as you're told!" Her tone brooked no objection. I went to my room and wearied myself trying to produce an irrefutable reason for my not being able to go. I even went so far as to wish I were Tom Sawyer or Huckleberry Finn with the ability to concoct a story with ease on the spot. Being discovered afterwards did not matter. Nothing came to mind. I rose earlier than usual next morning for my jog and on my return, I tried Mummy's door, but I could hear her having her devotions, so I quietly backed away. I still had time; visitation hours were from 11:00 a.m. to 1:00 p.m. Having showered and eaten my breakfast, I pulled up a chair near to Mummy who was seated at her sewing machine.

"Mummy, I don't want to go," I pleaded. "Can't you tell her I don't want to go?"

Mummy looked at me and said, "Your grandmother has her reasons for wanting you to go with her, so just go. Do you have anything else to do today?"

"No, but...."

"Well just go and be done with it."

That was it. I changed my clothes and was about to throw myself dejectedly into a chair when Granny appeared with some Gospel tracts and handed me a pile.

"Put those in your bag," she instructed, "and let's go."

"Gone, Mummy," I muttered.

"We should be back oneish," Granny informed Mummy. "Child, fix your face! You won't like it if it stayed like you have it now. Come on." With that, Granny shoved me through the door and shut it behind her.

I was thinking this had to be the worst day of my life. Really.

I still couldn't think of a reason for not wanting to go except that I didn't want to go. They both knew that I had no defense so with ill grace, I gave in and put my face the way I would prefer it to remain.

One van took us to Little Tokyo, and we walked to the hospital, arriving just after eleven o'clock.

"Good timing." Granny checked her watch approvingly.

We went straight to the Children's Ward first. I imagined that the really sick ones were those in bed with a parent or some other relative hovering at their side. Two were attached to drips of some sort and were dragging the contraption with them as they moved from one section to another. One or two were sitting around in the few chairs available, and a couple were on the swings outside, also with a parent or guardian. One bed was screened off from the rest of the children. They seemed to be in good spirits for the most part, but I couldn't see how they could be, given their conditions. I wanted to stay in the garden, in the fresh air. Granny chatted with the parents or guardians and the children who would respond, then gave them tracts and suggested that they read them to their children.

From Children's Ward, we went to Male Surgical and Male Medical. Thankfully, Granny told me to wait outside while she went in with her tracts. Next, we went to Female Surgical, Female Medical and Maternity Ward. On each ward Granny shared tracts and prayed with the patients and by the time we were ready to leave the place I had surrendered almost all my tracts, but I was in possession of a daunting appreciation of sickness and suffering and a lasting impression of our main hospital. In no way did the reality of that hospital meet the perception of hospital that I had developed from reading and from television. In each ward there had been a few empty beds and in each ward there was evidence of neglect and disrepair. Although there were window panes that needed replacing, ventilation was poor; vinyl tiles had formed themselves into a pattern of some here and some not here, and the nurses looked tired. The waiting area outside the wards, though breezy, needed a thorough scrubbing and the whole structure was bawling for a coat of paint.

I had been holding my breath most of the time and I had not spoken a word throughout the entire visitation, restricting my communication to a nod now and then. As we approached the gate once more, I glanced at my watch. It was 12:45 p.m.

Leading the way, Granny turned and cheerfully asked, "Well, that wasn't so bad after all, was it?"

Tears welled in my eyes as I struggled to stem the wave of nausea that assailed me. Bile gathered in my mouth. My stomach heaved. I retched and vomited. Granny barely escaped the deluge. I retched again and the rest of my breakfast became manure for the ixoras blooming in the garden near the gate. Grabbing me by the waist and mopping my eyes and face with her clean handkerchief, Granny hissed, "You see why all young ladies should walk with a clean 'kerchief?" And then she added, "Come along now."

She led me to the car park located across the road from the hospital and asked the attendant for some water so I could rinse my mouth. It was then that I started breathing normally again.

"Are you all right now?" Granny asked, and although I could hear the concern in her voice, I found myself muttering, "I told you I didn't want to come."

When the attendant returned with the water, I went to the end of the building and swished out my mouth and then rejoined Granny. As we thanked her, the attendant hesitated before extending an opened packet of Big Red and asking if I would like some chewing gum. I gratefully accepted a strip.

"I don't like hospitals," I tried explaining.

"I don't blame you," she responded.

We thanked her again and proceeded in silence to Tokyo to get a van back home.

After I had brushed my teeth and showered, I stayed in my room intending to reflect on my morning's experience. However, I must have fallen asleep because I woke with a start when I felt the presence of someone on my bed. Mummy reached out and patted my foot.

"What happened?"

"I'm not sure, but I know I shouldn't have gone."

"Well, you're okay again, so don't go making your granny feel worse than she does already."

"Well . . . yes," I had started when Granny appeared at the door. She came in and looked me over pensively.

"Look, I'm sorry, Vaughna. How was I to know you would get sick?" Granny said looking genuinely worried.

"I'll survive," I declared. "I'm better already. As a matter of fact, I'm getting up now," I added, swinging my legs to the floor. "And we could cross out nursing as a career."

"Looks so," Granny agreed. "I made some tri-tri cakes so you could have some with your provision or fish, unless you prefer bread," she offered leading the way to the kitchen. "You must be hungry."

Mummy sighed as she followed us. I settled for the tri-tri cakes with provision and fish and took my plate out to the porch. It was dusk already but I didn't turn on the lights so I could see out without being seen. Courtney Audain was sitting on their front steps eating roast corn, it looked like. I wondered idly where he had been this time, then concentrated on enjoying my food.

I could smell mint brewing for tea. About Courtney's exploits I would hear some time later, I was sure.

## Chapter Twenty-Five

Tedica came over and we started drafting application letters. She put hers on a thumb drive and emailed a copy to herself and I emailed mine to myself and kept a copy on my desktop waiting for our results so we could fill in the gaps.

The same day, Cousin Morrison and Phillippe came by with news of the house.

"I am going to change the face of the house and also do some construction at the back so I could have a split-level cottage-looking structure without going to an upstairs," he explained.

Phillippe groaned. "You know that means more work and less leisure for me!" he grimaced.

"Actually, I'm planning on getting a colleague, Ted, to work along with me," Cousin Morrison responded. "I have already discussed the architect's plan with him, so I'll confirm and get him here."

"I'll come in and look around one day when I go to church," Granny promised.

"Let me know so I could give you a 'before' view and 'after' view. We are going to need some workmen so if you know any good masons and carpenters, you could send them over." Cousin Morrison certainly seemed to have things under control.

"Well, maybe we could spend a day on the beach before the real work starts and before August Monday holiday," I suggested.

"Great!" Phillippe whooped. "A picnic! Now you're talking!"

Cousin Morrison shook his head with a wry smile while Mummy laughingly suggested that that may be a good way to recruit some labourers.

"Vaughna knows some unemployed youngsters who might just be willing."

I was already thinking of Rodney, Dave and Richie.

"Sure," I agreed. "I bet holding a piece of board or mixing some cement for a small change beats doing nothing any day!"

************

With so much going on around me, it was difficult to establish exactly when I became aware that something was amiss at the Audains'. I subsequently remembered that apart from that brief sighting of Courtney on their steps, I really had not seen much of them recently. I made the observation one morning in transit to another bite of my bakes. Sensing that Mummy and Granny had exchanged glances, I became alert.

"What...?" I started, but was interrupted by Mummy's,

"Claire is not well; hasn't been well for a good while now."

"What's wrong with her?" I wanted to know.

"The tests she's done so far don't show anything wrong with her," Granny responded.

"Well …. I'm confused," I admitted, totally puzzled. "Is she in pain?"

"No pain; just not well."

"So she's in bed?"

"Sometimes."

"I don't understand."

"We don't understand either, but that's the way it is," Mummy said in a tone of finality.

"Okay," I conceded, and I recalled my own "melancholy fit." I liked Claire, so I empathized with her although I knew I couldn't offer to go visit. I silently wished her well.

The next couple of days were really busy with demolition, construction, and planning the pre-emancipation holiday picnic. All those activities swished by in a whirl and then it was time for YPs camp in Grenada. We travelled to the Spice Isle by plane, but we returned by boat, island hopping to Carriacou, then to Union Island and then to mainland on a Thursday afternoon. We were all exhausted after ten days of fun and fellowship with our Grenadian and St. Lucian neighbours. I believe it is safe to say that all the returning campers slept for the whole day Friday.

Saturday morning, I awoke at the usual hour, but I decided to luxuriate in my bed after having slept in a sleeping bag for ten nights. So, by the time I appeared to have breakfast and begin my chores starting with washing the camp clothes, Granny and Mummy were well into their Saturday morning. The first load of clothes was just in the machine when I thought I heard Claire's voice next door. I raced to the living room window and sure enough, Claire was on Glenda's porch, and she wasn't alone. Wilmoth was with her, his left arm securing her to him at the waist. I could hardly contain myself. By the time they called Granny and Mummy I was at the front door and joining them before Granny could consider sending me away.

"Hi Claire, good to see you up and about," Granny's smile extended to them both. "Wilmoth."

"Miss Matt," was Wilmoth's beaming greeting.

Claire was smiling broadly, and Wilmoth looked as though he had just heard that he had won a couple million dollars.

"Well, Miss Matt, since I told you when Wilmoth broke my heart, I come to tell you that I have forgiven him."

"That is really good news," Granny smiled in approval.

"To tell the truth, I can't tell what was wrong with me the last few months, and the doctors can't say either, but Wilmoth was so attentive to me all the while, it would be heartless to not forgive him. I love him still." She leaned her head on his chest as he pulled her closer to him.

"Thanks for everything, Miss Matt. We going next door now."

Water was glistening in Wilmoth's eyes as he buckled his wife closer to him, if that were possible, and they went down the steps and started calling out to the neighbours. While surreptitiously trying to wipe away the tears from my eyes I noticed Mummy by the door doing the same thing.

# *Chapter Twenty-Six*

The final week of August rolled around and rumours abounded every day that results were out. Phillippe got his results first and passed all his 'A' Levels – Cambridge English, Sociology, Maths and Physics - with really good grades. Cousin Morrison paid him early so he could celebrate with his new friends.

Our 'A' Levels were a combination of CAPE and Cambridge. Communication Studies, English Literature, Spanish and Caribbean Studies were CAPE while Psychology and Geography were Cambridge. When results did come out, we all passed all our subjects. The boys looked like they were in the running for scholarships and we were not far behind. Since we had not heard the results of the other students, we had another time of waiting to endure. Tedica, DeDe, Avril, Lenora and I printed our letters of application and mailed them.

Having dispensed with the anxiety over passing our exams, we continued working on Cousin Morrison's house and watching it evolve into his West Indian dream cottage. For me there was a certain familial pride attached to the whole venture.

I had kept Dell and Tessa up-to-date with all my activities and events of the village, so now I had a matter to accost Dell about.

She was holding out on me! Did she really think I wouldn't find out? That long distance relationship was thriving like a weed! When I cornered her, I wanted to be able to drag every bit of information out of her. The appropriate occasion didn't make itself available because Glenda showed up at home with one of her 'creations' and before I knew it, I was literally conscripted to baste fabric in place and then tie and snip the threads when the sewing was done.

Glenda dreamed up these fancy ideas for drapes, made a sketch of them and came for Mummy to do the cutting and sewing. I would have preferred the option of doing whatever I could over at Cousin Morrison's but Glenda couldn't wait to see how her design would turn out, so she had almost set up camp at home. As soon as she returned from work on afternoons, she would pass in to 'see how things were going.' She knew that Mummy couldn't concentrate on her drapes to the exclusion of all else, but she made regular visits to ensure that she was not being ignored all together. Apart from having her house well "put away" Glenda was considering opening 'a little business' as she called it and she was trying to interest Mummy. I was mentally evaluating the possibilities as Glenda explained.

"Of course, we would do this legally with a proper contract from a reputable lawyer and all," she went on enthusiastically.

"No, not Lawyer Smith, even if he wasn't in the hospital," she joked.

"In hospital?" Mummy queried, obviously unaware of this development.

Glenda looked at Mummy in disbelief. "I can't believe you didn't hear about it! He in hospital calling list! And so he getting visitors!"

"Calling list?" I asked.

Now I was the focus of attention: Mummy's as she tried to quell my questioning with a look and Glenda's to provide what she thought was an explanation.

"Yes, well I went yesterday and he talked about the land in Fair Hall that he got from a Mrs. Clovis for two dollars a square foot in payment for doing some land business for her, and sold the same piece of land for nine dollars per square foot!"

"No!" Mummy objected.

"Uh huh! And then he started talking about a Miss Thomas and a Mr. Hutchins who he had charged fifteen thousand dollars, for settling out of Court, a dispute about some slander. Of the fifteen thousand, he gave Miss Thomas five thousand dollars and kept the rest for himself and told her that that was all Mr. Hutchins was willing to pay. The woman had already paid him to take the matter to Court."

I was wide-eyed and mute.

"We could see he had more to talk about, but the same time the latest wife rushed in breathless saying that he needs to rest so thanks for visiting and if we could oblige."

"I don't understand why people have to be so dishonest," Mummy admitted.

"The world is made up of all kinds," Glenda observed. "So what you think?"

It took me a while to realize that she was back to the business of the drapes. Mummy said she would think about it and let her know. When Glenda left and before I could ask again, Mummy explained that when wicked people are about to die, they have been known to confess their wicked deeds, and that is referred to as 'calling list'.

Mummy and I were in the kitchen, almost finished cooking when Granny returned from wherever she had been.

"I passed in at the hospital when I heard that Smith was there calling list," she said getting a glass of water from the pipe. (Granny never drank water from the fridge. "Juice is juice and water is water," was her explanation.)

"If the man is calling list, someone should share the Gospel with him. Maybe he would repent before he dies!"

"So you got to witness to him?" I had to ask.

"No. The wife was there, but she wasn't letting anybody talk to him. She had his chin tied up to keep his mouth shut."

"So he's dead?" Mummy wanted to know. The account didn't sound accurate. He couldn't be dead and still on the ward with Mrs. Smith keeping guard.

"No," Granny responded.

"But I thought it's only the mouths of dead people are tied up to make sure that they are not open when rigor mortis sets in," Mummy observed, puzzlement in her voice.

"Well, she tied up his chin to prevent him from talking when she wasn't there. He was also struggling to free himself of the straps that held him to the bed, preventing him from escaping."

"Oh! Well then, he's surely alive."

"Seems so!"

Now that I had processed all that information I started wondering if the Marshalls' name would get called and if Lawyer Smith were to die, whether they would ever get their money. I guessed that the former very much depended on Lawyer Smith himself, and the latter would eventually be determined by the law courts. And with that thought it crossed my mind that I had never heard of a lawyer being taken to Court. How does one deal with dishonesty on the part of a member of that profession?

After lunch I went to the village Post Office and collected a number of letters bearing my name. I knew they couldn't all be inviting me for an interview and immediately became despondent.

For a few days I moped about the house and then on Sunday in church, the Sunday School Superintendent appealed for volunteers to assist with teaching the Primary Girls and Intermediate Boys as the teachers for those classes were going abroad to study. I was sitting with my friends, but I sensed Granny's gaze in my direction and then I felt the unmistakably piercing intensity of Mummy's focus at the back of my neck. "*What now?*" was my immediate rebellious thought. I managed to avoid them after church, but at Sunday lunch, they effectively and literally tabled the subject.

"You should consider helping out," Granny started.

"Sounds like the current Assistant Teacher will become the class teacher and do most of the teaching. You would just have to help the children with their workbooks and so," Mummy added.

"I guess I could give it a try," I conceded. "But don't I have to be baptized to do that sort of thing in church?"

Both Mummy and Granny looked at me the same way, eyebrows raised quizzically.

"All right! All right! I'll talk to the Pastor." I ate the rest of my food in thoughtful silence.

That afternoon I went to look for Tedica. She had been assisting in her Sabbath School before 'A' Levels.

"You know we never thought about applying for a teaching job," I observed.

Tedica was shaking her head. "I did at one time, but we got so involved with the other applications that that idea just lost traction," she admitted with a pained expression.

"Well, don't you think we should?"

"I think the procedure is to write a letter to the Ministry of Education and send a copy of that same letter to Service Commissions along with their application form."

"Well, let's do the letters and get the application forms tomorrow."

We set to work on the appropriate wording for a letter for a job as a teacher and then I persuaded Tedica to let me peruse her copy of her Sabbath School Teacher's Manual. I am not certain what I expected, but I found the material very interesting.

As planned, we submitted our letters both to Service Commissions and to the Ministry of Education. I had called DeDe, Avril and Lenora to let them know about our decisions and they were going to submit letters for the teaching profession as well. Natalia was waiting for documentation from her Auntie Fay in Canada. She was supposed to start College in Montreal in January, so she was not seeking a permanent position.

By the middle of October we all received favourable responses from Service Commissions. Tedica was to report to Belair Primary; DeDe was to go to Marriaqua Primary; Avril was to go to Kingstown Anglican; Lenora was sent to Richmond Hill Government, and I was assigned to Sion Hill Government.

So, I had lots to share with Dell and Tessa. The sudden change of events had catapulted me from a state of unemployment to one of Primary School Teacher. Added to that, I, along with five other young people from YPs, was baptized by immersion the last Sunday in October and we were admitted to the membership of the church the same night.

Mummy and Granny were quietly observing me, first of all preparing the Activity for my Primary Girls class at church and then poring over Schemes of Work to prepare for my Junior 3 class at school. I knew that meant they were praying for me. It was a good feeling.

## Chapter Twenty-Seven

After I had updated Dell and Tessa, I had to challenge Dell.

"So how are the holiday plans progressing?" I asked on SKYPE so that I could read every nuance of her response. I was determined to drag some admission out of my sister.

Dell smiled. "What holiday plans?" she hedged.

"The same ones that are causing you to smile," I stated. "You might as well fess up because I know."

"And since you know, why are you asking?" The girl was still smiling.

"For confirmation," I replied. "You could at least keep me in the know. I tell you everything!"

"But you know already! Okay. We are planning to have Steven come to England and we are going on a European tour," she stated.

"We?"

"Vaughna, you know that neither Mummy and Granny nor Uncle Marcus and Auntie Annesta would hear of my going on a two-week European holiday alone with Steven."

"So?"

"Andrew and Sonia are going, a Filipino and a Bajan from my class, Elena and Steven, seven of us."

"How many males and how many females?"

"Three males; four females. The Filipino is a male."

"How are you organizing accommodation?" my practical mind wanted to know.

"Andrew and Sonia are taking care of that and we have so far each secured funds for travel expenses."

"Okay!" I approved. I smiled too as I remembered the pact that Tessa and I had made. We would have a holiday of our own minus all the complications of the planned European tour!

"I presume Granny and Mummy have already been told all the details."

"Yes. Uncle Marcus and Auntie Annesta discussed it with them. But you know that! Why are you asking me about things that you have the answers to already? Mummy and Granny must have told you."

"Actually, they did mention it but the finer points I gleaned elsewhere."

"Well, who from?"

I pretended I hadn't heard her. Have to keep some cards close to the chest! I didn't have to ask her when because I knew those plans were for next summer. Two could play at the same game. She was looking at me and shaking her head when I flippantly said, "Got to go. Have some lessons to plan!"

Finally, the announcement about the Island scholarships was made. Rodney got one of the two Island Scholarships, so he was going to study Civil Engineering next school year. Meanwhile, he had found a job at CWSA. The rest of us were going to keep in close contact with Service Commissions so we could apply for the first scholarships that were posted. For the time being, we were making the most of our teaching experiences.

I was almost home one afternoon of the last week of the first term of school when a long silver-grey car crawled past me in the slow-moving traffic. Lawyer Smith was on the passenger side of his vehicle driven by his son. He looked poorly, but he was alive.

Granny was the first person I met at home.

"I just saw Lawyer Smith in his car with his son."

"Yes, it seems he is recuperating."

"Isn't that going to prove rather embarrassing after all that confessing?" I wanted to know.

"We could look at it another way. He's been given an opportunity to make amends," Granny advised.

"Hmm .... I guess we'll see what he does with it." Immediately my imagination conjured up visions of Lawyer Smith calling a public meeting and handing over a cheque to Mrs. Clovis, and then the lady who was slandered would be called up for her cheque of the outstanding ten thousand dollars, followed by the two children who were swindled out of their inheritance. He was returning the deed to their property. The Marshalls would get a cheque for their money with interest. And so on and so forth. Before I knew it, I had spoken my thoughts.

"And pigs would fly!"

"Don't be so cynical, Vaughna. People can change. That's what salvation does to a person."

I was too hungry to engage Granny in an argument that I was sure to lose anyway, so I gave up.

## *Chapter Twenty-Eight*

Cousin Morrison's house was finished. The barricades had been removed, the front and back yard landscaped and the quaint fence that provides a measure of privacy had been erected. The transformation of the structure that was there before was just unbelievable. Traffic slowed so the drivers and passengers could get as much a look as possible. The pastel green on the walls blended into a soft blue on the decorated fascia board and the porch ceiling. Bronze bay windows lent an air of sophistication to the front house and the semi-surround verandah was positioned to capture the breeze yet shelter the front rooms from weather. Cousin Morrison and Ted had really put their engineering and architectural expertise to work and had achieved their goal. The four bedrooms were large and breezy, the master bedroom, every homeowner's dream. While I liked the master bedroom with its well-appointed spaces, the kitchen and dining room had me totally fascinated. I didn't know much about layout and floor planning, but I found the crafty utilization of space remarkable. Fixtures and appliances fitted into their spaces with perfection and gave the rooms a very clean and comfortable appearance. I don't know how they managed it, but the living room and den were also spacious, the one flowing naturally into the other. The laundry was in a world of its own.

It was discreetly located in a space that accommodated washer, dryer, a sink, shelves for laundry supplies and a freezer. The house was just one amazing utilization of space and an expression of understated luxury. I knew that Jessica and Flora would be ecstatic when they came for Christmas. To look at Phillippe when we did the "After" walkthrough, one would believe he was responsible for the architectural accomplishment.

Obviously, Christmas dinner was going to be at the house. Cousin Morrison had asked the Pastor to pronounce the blessing on the home the Sunday before. Christmas was the next Thursday.

Tedica and the boys were coming to the blessing which was to be followed by a backyard barbecue; Christmas dinner was for family.

The chief mason donned an apron in an affirmation of his assertion that he was the best person at a barbecue pit. Cousin Morrison decided that he was going to rise to the challenge, so he too garbed up in an apron. Cousin Flora put an end to the friendly rivalry by declaring that she had seasoned all the meat, so any credit for the taste of the barbecue was rightfully hers. Thoroughly chastened, the men agreed to shelve the competition until another occasion and work together. Jessica and I were at the kitchen counter making sure that the potato salad was just as

Cousin Flora wanted it while she laid out the cutlery and crockery on the marble topped concrete table, constructed in the yard for just such an occasion.

"Our Phillippe seems to be enjoying himself," Jessica observed as his youthful laughter could be heard from across the yard. He, along with Tedica, Richie, Rodney and Dave was lounging close to the trestle table and seat not far from the barbecue pit. "I hope he remembers that he's down for washing up!"

"Don't worry. Can't you see he has plenty help?"

The barbecue was all that I had expected it to be. The breadfruit was the right texture and taste; the portions of pork and chicken were exceptional in taste and quantity; our potato salad met Cousin Flora's rigid standards and Granny's fruit punch was beyond compare. The company was good too. We had so much fun recounting tales of the building experience that Cousin Morrison decided that he had to have that recorded. He was going to open an album with the construction journey and include the narratives. Phillippe volunteered himself and Tedica to do the formatting and I winked at Jessica. When Tedica had passed on the information about Dell's European tour as she had received it from Ronald Dunbar, I was more than a bit concerned, but now it took great effort to mask the smile of satisfaction as I observed her and Phillippe. All was well.

\*\*\*\*\*\*\*\*\*\*\*\*\*\*\*\*\*\*\*\*\*\*\*\*\*\*\*\*

We still had food in our fridge on Tuesday, which was just as well because Mummy decided to use the three days before Christmas to completely ransack the house and put it to right again. The cushion covers were washed and put away and I was commissioned to put on the new ones. Everything in the China cabinet was taken out, washed, dried and packed away again. The cabinet itself was cleaned with vinegar while the glass was made sparkling with the application of Windex. I had to polish the wooden frame with the same O' Cedar polish that we used for the rest of the wooden furniture. Honestly, I thought Mummy was subconsciously trying to capture and transfer the newness of Cousin Morrison's house to ours. Before showering and falling into my bed on Christmas Eve night, I set up the Christmas tree as usual while Mummy put up the new curtains. Everybody's bed had new sheets and all the windows had different curtains. The house smelled of polish, bleach and disinfectant. Christmas! My one disappointment was that nobody came serenading.

As we were taking a dish to Cousin Morrison's, Mummy had planned to bake early in the morning. The kitchen was already smelling of newly baked bread when I crawled out of my bed.

"Merry Christmas!" I shouted from my bedroom door. "Merry Christmas" responses came from the kitchen, so I knew Granny and Mummy were both there. I sneaked their gifts under the tree then went to prepare myself to demolish that bread that was tantalizing me.

Normally, Christmas day was spent quietly at home, more so since the day disappeared so swiftly. Granny would remind us of the Christmas story from the Bible, then we would breakfast together, open presents and then help with preparing lunch. Christmas lunch was usually enough for Boxing Day lunch as well. On Boxing Day, we were allowed to visit friends or have friends come over to our place.

When I went out on the porch with my big fat balloon so I could look through it to see the rising sun dance, Glenda and Marlon were on their porch having breakfast. We exchanged Christmas greetings.

"Watching the sun dance, as usual," she observed. "Looks like we will get a little drizzle later, possibly this afternoon. Don't forget to come for some of my cake," she invited.

"I'll get it tomorrow maybe. We're going out today."

"Okay. Enjoy."

I thought about all the good food I had eaten recently and sighed. I would be bursting out of my clothes by the time I was ready to go back to work!

Christmas lunch left my palate tingling. I am unapologetically partial to Mummy's eggplant dish baked with garlic, parsley and plenty cheese, but the rest of the food was scrumptious.

After lunch, Jessica produced a pack of *Snap* and challenged Phillippe and me. She certainly had an eagle's eye and a "SNAP" voice that scared the cards right out of one's grasp!

By four o'clock we were back home and I headed straight for my bed. It was well past eight o'clock when I surfaced again. Dell and Tessa were ready with a report of their day and seeking a run-down of mine. I confessed that I was going to do nothing else but laze around for the next couple days and try not to eat anything unless I absolutely had to.

I felt that I had gained at least five pounds, and all in the wrong places so I crawled out of bed on Old Year's morning, donned my track suit, socks and sneakers as usual and did my lap around the yard before heading on to the road. Courtney Audain jumped off their porch wall and started for their front gate.

"Hi Vaughna!" he called.

By this time, I was about ten yards up the road. Out of the corner of my eye I saw him vault their fence and start up the road after me. I accelerated. He couldn't know the route I take. For no reason that I could lucidly explain, I determined that Courtney Audain was not catching me. I accelerated further without looking back. Having left the main road, I wound my way along the village road and then charged up the gouti track. Sure that I had lost Courtney, I slackened my pace along the other long stretch of village road and then cruised down the second gouti track. Arriving back on the village road I checked my watch.

Twenty three minutes. I was once more approaching the main road and the final stretch for home. No sign of Courtney. At an even pace, I jogged into the yard, made the lap around the house, checked my watch again and decided I could do another, and then ran up the six steps to the porch. Bending from the waist as our PE teacher had taught us in secondary school, I allowed my arms to hang limp as I breathed hard through my mouth.

Somewhere between breaths, I detected a slight sound. Raising my head in investigation, I watched Courtney Audain unfold his lanky frame from Granny's white-painted wrought iron porch chair.

"Can we talk now, Vaughna?" Extending both hands, Courtney bestowed on me a smile that competed with the early morning sunshine, and as our eyes met, the erratic thumping of my heart and the ragged breath struggling through my mouth and nose were not from exhaustion.

# Glossary

'Gouti' track: The name given to a narrow concrete village pathway.

Jumbie: Ghost; apparition; phantom; spectre

'Planning': Using the flat part of the cutlass to strike; striking someone with the flat part of the cutlass

Praying in the New Year: Prayers that begin in the final hours or minutes of the Old Year and continue into the first few minutes of the New Year.

Shirt tail: The end or loose part of the shirt that would normally be inserted in the pants

Skirt tail: The end part of the skirt that includes the hem

# *Review of Call it Our Village*

Vaughna Craigg's primarily adolescent first person narration of ***Call it Our Village***, is spread over a five to seven year period, with socio-historical flashbacks which provide context for the episodes in her suburban Arnos Vale Village.

Vaughna's worldview is shaped by her matrifocal Evangelical Christian setting, where Granny and Mummy are the foundation on which Vaughna and her big sister Dell are nurtured and bloom. Vaughna's bond with the demure Dell in no way suppresses Vaughna's own dogged personality which fuels the energy with which this story is told. Yet the Vaughna who had to be 'kept out of mischief' is mortally afraid of dogs and her story begins 'At the first sound of the menacing growl' which sent her '...flying downhill, determined not to be caught.' ***Call it Our Village*** is a fast-paced, very well-written novella which hugs its audience with a deft insightfulness into a contemporary Vincentian milieu, where lawyers are the main villains of the peace.

**Andrea Keizer-*Bowman***

B.A.Hons.UWI. (Literature with History);P.G.C.E. (English;History) University of London; M.A. (Language and Literature in Education) University of London; M.Phil. (Comparative Literature) Trinity College, Dublin.

Made in the USA
Middletown, DE
15 July 2024